complete guide

HOW TO SURVIVE FIFTH GRADE
AND THE APOCALYPSE

Summary: When strange lights appear over the Catskills, and
classmates begin disappearing, Doomy Prepper and his friends
must work together to save the town from an alien invasion.

BISAC: JUVENILE FICTION/Science Fiction/Alien Contact.
JUVENILE FICTION/Action & Adventure/Survival Stories.
JUVENILE FICTION/Social Themes/Friendship.
JUVENILE FICTION/Historical/United States/ 20th Century.
For more information about this title, write us at Mystery Goose
Press P.O. Box 86627 Vint Hill, VA 20187

Printed in the United States of America.
Library of Congress Control Number: 2019940947
Paperback ISBN: 978-1-948882-11-8
Also available as an ebook.

DOOMY PREPPER'S COMPLETE GUIDE

HOW TO SURVIVE FIFTH GRADE AND THE APOCALYPSE

AMIE BORST

Illustrated by

SEAN BOVA

Catskills, New York
October, 1986

CONTENTS

1. Obey The Rules   1
2. Keep Your Eye On The Sky   7
3. Choose Your Battles Wisely   12
4. Recruit A Friend Smarter Than You   17
5. Report Your Findings Before Your Sister Rats You Out   23
6. Prepare for the Apocalypse   30
7. Keep Your Nose Clean   36
8. Be A Team Player   42
9. Do Not Ignore Clues   51
10. Always Keep A Supply of Toilet Paper   58
11. Never Foil With Aluminum Foil   65
12. Try To Trick Your Substitute   72
13. Secure Permission Slips For Survival   77
14. Discover Your Code Words   84
15. Make Your Discoveries in Silence   90
16. Use All of Your Senses   96
17. Fool Proof Your Plan   105
18. Divide And Conquer   112
19. Never Submit To Zombification   120
20. Become A Morse Code Ninja   129
21. Be Smarter Than Your Average Tentacle   138
22. Defeat The Right Enemy   146
23. Never Trust An Alien That Says It Comes In Peace Unless You Want To Become Its Pieces   154
24. Never Take All The Credit   160

Acknowledgments   167
A Note From the Author   169
About the Author   171
About the Illustrator   173
Also by Amie Borst   175

OBEY THE RULES

EVERY FIFTH GRADER knows three very important things.

1. Don't trade sandwiches with Mikey Fuller. He always has tuna fish.
2. Never stare at Mrs. Nebula's mole, you'll turn into stone.
3. Always ignore the lights in the sky.

So, the first one was a rookie mistake. How was I supposed to know Mikey would have the smelliest sandwich on the planet? It's not like anyone warned me. Plus, he was the only one willing to trade for my MRE. That's short for Meals Ready to Eat, in case you didn't know. We have a ton of them. 17,520 to be exact. Dad says we need to be prepared for four whole entire years. You know, just in case there's an alien invasion. Or a zombie apocalypse. Like that would ever happen.

The second one was a rumor. I heard it from Mikey who heard it from Billy who heard it from his neighbor that Mrs. Nebula kept a statue of a kid in her living room. But we all know it's the boy from third grade. The one everyone claims moved away except we know that's just a cover story for what really happened. Mrs. Nebula turned him to stone. And then she kidnapped him. It's true! Everyone knows it. Especially since Mrs. Nebula was the last one to see him. Alive.

So, you can probably understand why I wasn't taking any chances when Mrs. Nebula asked us to turn in our papers.

"Class, please. I'm not asking again. Turn in your science homework." I glanced up just long enough to see Mrs. Nebula standing at her desk, tapping an empty corner where our morning work had been just seconds earlier. "Snip snap."

"Snap snip," someone echoed from the back of the room with a snicker. A few giggles followed.

"I heard that," Mrs. Nebula said, her back now turned to us as she dragged a piece of chalk across the board. It made that familiar awful screeching sound. The hairs on my arms stood on end.

I threw my hands up and covered my ears. "Ugh," I groaned, scrunching my face until I couldn't see.

"Is there a problem?" Mrs. Nebula snapped around.

"No." I shook my head. "I mean no, ma'am."

"Doomy. Front and center. Now." Mrs. Nebula slapped her ruler on her desk. Twhack, thwack, thwack.

"Yes, Mrs. Nebula." I inched out of my seat and marched to my doom, keeping my chin up and head held high. Might as well go to the gauntlet with a sense of pride. My eyes stared at the board behind her. It was dang near impossible not to look at that mole. It was the size of Mars. Plus, it had three long, dark hairs sticking out of it. I swear, sometimes they waved at me like she had a third arm on her cheek. I blinked away the water leaking from my eyes. That's when I realized I couldn't move. I was frozen!

Oh-my-heck! Mrs. Nebula had, in fact, turned me into stone!

I KNEW IT.

"What are you doing, Doomy?" Mrs. Nebula paused and squinted at me. "Do I need to send you to the principal's office?"

I wanted to respond, but I couldn't. How could I? I'd been turned to stone. Stone, I tell you!

"Doomsday Prepper. I'm speaking to you, young man."

"Mrs. Nebula," Peter's voice carried up to us from where he was seated at his desk.

"What is it, Peter?"

"Doomy doesn't look so good."

He was right. Stone doesn't look good on anyone! The whole class knew I had been made into a statue. Why couldn't Mrs. Nebula see that?

"Maybe he should go to the nurse."

Of course. The nurse! Peter was a genius.

Mrs. Nebula looked at me and I made a gagging face. I felt like I was going to hurl. "Doomy, stop playing games." Mrs. Nebula started coming at me, hands on her hips and lips pinched into a thin line.

I tried to speak, but nothing would come out.

"I'm talking to *you*."

"Uh, uh, uh," I groaned. My arm got a sudden itch and, even though I didn't think I could move, it was out of control. I reached over to scratch it except, instead, my hand swatted all the papers off her desk.

"That's it, Mister. To Principal Geller's office."

"But—"

"Now!"

My head and shoulders—now unfrozen from the mole-staring spell—slumped as I walked out of classroom 234.

You'd think my day couldn't get any worse, but then number three happened.

KEEP YOUR EYE ON THE SKY

EVERYONE KNEW ABOUT THE LIGHTS.

1. They had always been there.
2. We weren't allowed to talk about them.
3. They had never changed.

The lights changed at precisely 1:52 pm. So you can probably understand why I was very intrigued.

I wasn't really doing anything out of the ordinary when I noticed them flashing. In fact, it was my usual afternoon stroll. I was headed straight to the principal's office...after a brief detour to the courtyard. Normally, the lights were a steady burn of glowing white orbs floating in the sky (not that I'd peeked), so I had to look twice when I saw them change. They turned hot pink and flashed in a strobe-like pattern. At first, I thought maybe the Bee-Gee Brothers had returned with a bad case of disco fever, but when I opened the door and looked skyward, I knew this was something else entirely.

Cool air popped me in the face as I walked into the courtyard. The door slipped from my fingers and slammed shut with a loud thud. The sky was a haze of fluffy pink, like cotton candy straight from the carnival. Mom would have said it looked like a storm-sky, but I knew better. There was something different about this.

Something supernatural.

Something otherworldly.

Something extraterrestrial.

George Lucas would agree.

"Whoa," I said, staring wide-eyed into the sky. "No one's gonna believe this." Normally I'd take a Polaroid of something so spectacular, but I'd left my camera at home right next to my He-Man action figure collection. Skeletor was the coolest even if my

sister thought he was a stupid twerp. Kind of like her
boyfriend.

That's when Mrs. Stuffy McStuffkins (that's not
really her name but it should be) spoiled the fun.

"Doomy!" Mrs. Stewart, the hall monitor, yelled
as she stood in the doorway. She drilled a pencil into
her permed mullet with one hand and held the door
ajar with the other. "What are you doing out there?"

"Looking at the lights." I turned away and stared
up at the sky.

"You know you're not supposed to do that," Mrs.
Stewart whispered, her face going pale. "Get inside
before—"

"Why are you whispering?" I asked without blinking. "There's nothing to be afraid of. Besides, they're pink now." I scratched my head.

The hall-monitor gasped. "You know the rules!" She grabbed my arm and stared me down. "I don't want your excuses. Go back to class!"

"Oh, but I'm not going to class." I turned to face the open door. I couldn't miss a moment of the light show. How Mrs. Stewart could just ignore something so magical was beyond me. "I'm supposed to go to Principal Geller's office."

"Well, Doomy, you better get moving before I tell him to call your parents."

"Yes, Mrs. Stewart." I shuffled away from the picnic table, my eyes growing wide as the lights flashed twice. They changed from pink back to white. Then, suddenly, the lights went out completely. "That's strange. It's like it never even happened."

"Mrs. Stewart? Did you see that?" I couldn't take my eyes off the sky to find out. Good thing I didn't because the lights winked back on, one by one. They whirled before changing to a weird shade of green. "Wow!" I breathed the words in total awe.

"Doomsday!" Mrs. Stewart snapped. She held the door open as she tapped her foot.

Couldn't she see I was busy? "Yes?"

"Now!"

Keeping my eyes on the sky, I began to back away. A small crescent of silver blipped out of the cloud. Surely, Mrs. Stewart had seen it, too, but when I turned toward her, she had her eyes down. A sourpuss crossed her face as she folded her arms. By the time I glanced back at the sky, the mysterious silver crescent had already vanished.

CHOOSE YOUR BATTLES WISELY

YOU CAN COUNT on Principal Geller.

1. He always has a dish of candy on his desk.
2. You can have as many pieces as you want.
3. He gets to talk one minute for each piece of candy you take.

Even though he had my favorite chocolate, I decided I didn't really want to be in his office too long because I wanted to tell Peter about the lights. So, I only took one piece of candy. Two if you include the piece of Bazooka bubble gum.

"That's ten minutes," Principal Geller said. "Five minutes for each piece."

"But I thought..."

"Never mind what you thought, Doomy." Principal Geller pushed the candy bowl toward me. "Tell me why you're here."

I shrugged. "I mean, I guess Mrs. Nebula was upset that *she*..."

Principal Geller raised an eyebrow.

"Mrs. Nebula was upset that *I* was frozen." I bit

into the Milky Way bar and a wad of saliva dripped from my mouth. "You know. In fear."

"Frozen in fear, Doomy? From what?"

"Because she turns students into stone."

"Is that so?" Principal Geller folded his hands across his forehead hiding his eyes.

"Yeah. Everyone knows she froze that kid in third grade."

"You mean Matthew Mahoney?"

I shrugged again as I shoved the last bite of the candy into my mouth. "I don't know his name but if you say so, then I guess that's him."

"Matthew moved away at the end of the school year."

I leaned forward across the desk and whispered, "Well, that's what they want us to believe." I pointed back and forth between the principal and me. "But we know better, don't we Principal Geller?"

The principal rubbed his forehead. "Look, Doomy, you've got to stop disrupting class. And you have to stop making up these stories. Last time it was something about a zombie."

"Mummy."

"Oh right, he left a trail of toilet paper down the hall."

"She."

"She?"

"Yes. Everyone knows that mummies are girls."

"And I suppose zombies are boys."

"Don't be silly, Principal Geller," I laughed as I

reached for the piece of Bazooka. I shoved it in my mouth, chomping into it. "Deadies are boys."

"Of course. Everyone knows that."

"Can I go now?" I stood up.

"Not so fast. I think it's time we doled out a punishment, don't you?"

"Punishment? For what?"

"For your behavior."

"But...but..." The lamp on Principal Geller's desk flickered. My eyes grew wide as I thought about the weird stuff I'd seen in the sky. "Did you know the lights can change color?"

"What lights, Doomy?"

"The ones in the sky."

Principal Geller gasped. Just like Mrs. Stewart had. All the adults in this town were just as afraid of the lights as the kids were. "Go back to class, Doomy."

Before leaving, I swiped another piece of candy from his dish.

"I saw that, Mister. You owe me an additional five minutes next time you're here."

"What makes you think I'll be back?"

"You're always back, Doomy."

He was right. I was there at least once a day. But things were going to be different. People were going to start believing me. Beginning with my best friend, Peter.

RECRUIT A FRIEND SMARTER THAN YOU

PETER PETERSON IS the best friend I could ever ask for.

1. He believed me. No matter what.
2. He could keep a secret.
3. He always scored 100% on all of his tests.

"Ninety-six?" Peter looked at his paper in disgust.

Last Friday we'd taken a quiz on the solar system. Peter had helped me study, so I was hoping for a decent grade. Even though I hadn't yet reached my desk, I could see the big red blemish from a mile away.

"Sixty-eight?" I sunk into my seat.

Peter leaned forward and tapped on my shoulder. "Didn't you borrow my flashcards?"

I shrugged. "Yeah."

"Did you use them?"

I swung around in my seat to face Peter. "Ugh," I said with another shrug.

"Osmosis doesn't work with studying, dude." Peter tucked his paper into a folder and filed it inside his desk.

My cheeks flushed. "I'd argue that, but I don't know what osmosis means."

"It was in the unit before last," Peter said.

"Well how was I supposed to know that?"

"C'mon, Doomy. Everyone knows that."

"I bet they don't know about the lights."

Peter pushed his much-too-big glasses from the tip of his nose back toward his eyes. "Everyone knows about the lights, Doomy." He did his weird wink thing to settle the frames into place.

"But do they know they change color?" I'm pretty sure I raised my eyebrow. I'd been practicing in the mirror at home and had nearly saved it to muscle memory.

"Color?" Peter leaned forward.

"Ah ha! See? You didn't know."

"Shhhh...."

"You should have seen it, Peter! They changed to pink and were flashing and then they were green and then—"

"Zip it." Peter pulled his fingers across his lips then clamped his mouth shut.

"It was the coolest thing ever!"

Peter shook his head with his lips pinched tight. He grabbed a pencil from his pouch and opened a notebook. He stared down at his desk.

What *I* didn't know was that Mrs. Nebula had walked up behind me. "Doomy Prepper."

I whirled around in my seat. "Mrs. Nebula!"

She stood there with her arms crossed as she tapped her foot on the floor. The long, black hairs on her mole waved at me. I blinked, convinced she'd turn me into stone again. "Disrupting class are we, Doomy?"

"N...n...no, ma'am."

"Good." Her eyes darted to the exam on my desk with the big sixty-eight written at the top in bright red ink. "Then see me after class."

As she turned to walk away, the school bell rang.

"Phew," I said, breathing a sigh of relief. I sunk back into my seat.

Peter tapped my shoulder. "I believe you, Doomy."

I turned to face him and watched as he neatly filed his papers into three separate folders. I crammed mine into my bag. "You do?"

"Of course. But I don't think you should go around announcing these stories. People are weird."

"Yeah, I guess you're right." I slipped my bag over my shoulder. "Wanna come over and play Asteroids?"

"Maybe after I finish my homework. Big project due." Peter headed for the door. "Don't you have to work on it, too?"

"Oh yeah, right. I guess so." Why was there always so much homework? The timing couldn't be worse, either. Things were just getting interesting! I'd rather be investigating the lights instead of working on some time-sucking project. "See you later, then?"

"Sure." Peter waved as he started out the door.

I was only one step behind him when Mrs. Nebula grabbed my shoulder. "Not so fast, young man."

My breath caught in my throat.

"We're going to have a discussion. Just the two of us."

"I'd love to have a discussion with you, Mrs. Nebula, but you see I have to get home to my sister. She has—"

"Let me guess." Mrs. Nebula cleared her throat. "The flu? Chicken pox? A weird virus that turns her hair purple?"

"Actually, it's pink."

Peter laughed and Mrs. Nebula twisted on her heel to face him. "Excuse me?" She shook her finger.

While Mrs. Nebula's back was turned, I nodded

at Peter and then tapped my watch. He motioned back.

Mrs. Nebula whirled around and stared down her nose at me. "I was going to give you a second chance on that exam but now I think I'll just make it a permanent red mark in the grade book."

While most kids would have thought that was pretty bad, and maybe even felt threatened by it, I smiled. Even though I'd failed the test, that sixty-eight might actually bring my grade up. "Alright-y then. I'll catch you tomorrow."

"I'm not done with you."

"You're not?" I tried not to stare at her, but it wasn't easy. My eyes seemed fixated on the mole on her cheek. "Need me to help you grade papers?" I fished a purple marker out of my pocket and uncapped the top. Ink leaked onto my hands. "I can do them in a jiffy."

Mrs. Nebula sighed heavily. "Never mind, Doomy. Go home."

REPORT YOUR FINDINGS BEFORE YOUR SISTER RATS YOU OUT

MY SISTER WILL DO a few things every time I tell her a story.

1. Turn up her Walkman.
2. Ignore me.
3. Tell me to go away.

"Tell me more!" My sister took off her headphones.

"Well, the lights changed color. They were white, then they turned pink, and then they were green!"

"The lights were pink and green? For real?" My sister's eyes grew wide.

I stepped closer. "For real!"

My sister gasped. "I don't believe it."

"But you have to believe me, Gabby."

"I don't have to believe anything you say. And don't call me that." She shoved me out and slammed the door. "Now go away, you little twerp."

I burst back into her room. "No really. The lights were pink!"

"I told you to GO A-WAY." She belly-flopped onto her bed.

"Fine." I swiped her Duran Duran cassette tape off her dresser. "But don't say I didn't warn you." I waved the tape over my head as I started to back out of her doorway.

"Hey, that's mine." My sister leapt off her bed and bolted across the room. "Give it back."

I slammed the door and pulled the handle so she couldn't open it. "Not until you promise to listen."

"Fine."

"You swear?" My grip loosened and she yanked the door open.

"Yeah, I swear." The music sang through her headphones, which still hung around her neck like a necklace. I tipped my head and she sighed before clicking off her Walkman. "I'm listening. Now give it to me."

"Oh no. Story first, then I'll release your precious Duran Duran."

"Ma-um," my sister shouted over the railing.

"What Gabrielle?"

"Doomy's holding Duran hostage again!"

"Good grief, Doomy. How many times do I have to tell you to leave your sister's things alone?"

"Fine." I tossed the tape at her. "Forget about it."

My sister fumbled the catch and the tape clattered to the floor. After she picked it up, she crossed one leg in front of the other. Her neon green leg warmers looked like giant caterpillars. They ate her ankles as she leaned against the wall with her arms crossed.

I huffed and started walking down the hall toward my bedroom.

"Did you really see the lights change?"

I stopped in my tracks and held my breath.

"Because I heard from Molly who heard from Teresa who heard it from Brad that someone in his sixth period gym class saw something in the sky during his lunch break."

"Was it silver?" I asked, still holding my breath, my shoulders tight to my ears.

"I don't know, but apparently Brad said the kid was pretty freaked."

"Because I saw something silver." I turned around, my cheeks flushing with each step as I approached my sister. "It shot out of the clouds and back again."

"Really?" My sister stared at me.

"Uh-huh. And then—"

"Don't repeat this, Doomy—but Brad said this kid saw little green men coming out of the spaceship."

My jaw dropped to the ground. "I knew it! Aliens!"

"I'm just messing with you, twerp." She ruffled my hair.

Pop. Gabby totally burst my bubble. "You're such a jerk."

"Oh c'mon. You didn't really believe any of that, did you?"

"No," I said, heat flushing my cheeks.

My sister laughed as she slammed her bedroom door. "Don't let the aliens get you," she shouted.

"I'm sure *you'll* be fine," I said staring at her bedroom door plastered with posters. "I hear aliens actually prefer people with brains."

"What was that?" Dad's voice came from behind.

I whirled around.

"Doomy." Dad studied his salt and pepper mustache in the hallway mirror.

"Huh?" I said with a gulp.

"Something about preferring brains. Talking about zombies again, Doomy?"

I laughed as I let out the breath I was holding. "Yeah, something like that."

"You've got quite the imagination there, young man." Dad puffed his chest as he straightened his posture.

"Whatever." But that's not what this was. Not at all. This wasn't just another story. It was true. And I wanted someone other than Peter to believe me.

"Everything okay, Doomy?"

I shrugged. "I guess."

"Dinner's in ten minutes." He ruffled my hair. "Meatloaf. And I don't mean the singer." Dad laughed at his own joke.

I went to my room and kicked back on my bed, staring up at the ceiling. Something weird was happening and I was going to figure it out.

"Time for dinner!" Mom called.

As soon as I sat at the table, Mom passed the mashed potatoes. "Anything interesting happen at school today, Doomy?"

I took the bowl and served myself three heaping spoonfuls. Shoveling in a mouthful, I said, "Not really."

Mom spread a napkin across her lap. "That's not what I heard."

My cheeks puffed out as I held the potatoes in my mouth.

"I got a call from Principal Geller."

I coughed and the potatoes flew back onto my plate.

"Not another call, Doomy." Dad shook his head. "This has really got to stop." He stabbed his fork into a slab of ketchup-covered meat.

"I bet I know what it was about this time," my sister said.

Dad concentrated on his plate of food. "And what would that be?"

My sister smirked at me as she said, "The lights."

PREPARE FOR THE APOCALYPSE

MY DAD HAS some good traits.

1. He's a doctor.
2. Homework is his specialty.
3. He can stay as cool as a cucumber,
   especially under pressure.

Dad's knuckles blanched as he held his fork in his right hand. "Why would Principal Geller be calling us about the lights, Doomy?" He slammed his other hand on the table.

My mashed potatoes didn't look appetizing anymore. I dragged my fork through them making railroad tracks.

"Doomy, I'm talking to you," Dad growled through clenched teeth.

"Because Mrs. Nebula was upset that *she*...I mean, *I* was—"

"Hold on a second here, buddy. There's more to this story?"

"There's always more." My sister took a swig from her can of soda.

"Shut up, *Gabrielle*."

"Don't talk to your sister like that." Mom was carefully loading her fork with the perfect bite of food, which included a sampling of everything on her plate. A stubborn pea fell off her fork for a second time. She rolled it with her knife into her potatoes. It stuck there like glue before she shoved the bite into her mouth. "More potatoes?" Mom handed me the bowl.

My stomach churned. "She's lucky I didn't call her Blabby Gabby like I wanted to."

"Doomy!" Mom said as she gave me the side-eye.

"Never mind the story." Dad leaned forward and took a sip of coffee. "Just tell us what you told Principal Geller about the lights."

I couldn't remember the exact wording, but I tried my best. "They changed color. Flashed pink and lit up the sky."

"Pink?" Dad's coffee leapt out of his mouth onto his dinner plate.

"Looked like cotton candy straight from the carnival. You shoulda seen it."

Mom handed him a napkin. "You all right, honey?"

"Fine. Fine." Dad swiped the napkin across his lips and dried up the excess that crept into his peas. "Is that all, Doomy?"

I wanted to tell him about the silver thing, too, but—

"He saw something shiny," my sister said with a smirk. "Or was it silver?"

I gave her the stink eye.

"Bet he thinks it was a spaceship." My sister twirled a strand of her bleached blonde hair around her finger.

"I never said that!"

Gabby put her feet up on the table. "You didn't have to."

"Excuse me, missy. Put your feet down." Mom assembled another perfect bite but paused long enough to narrow her eyes at my sister. "I'm sure it was just an airplane. Right, Doomy?" Mom chewed her food at least a hundred times.

"Would you stop doing that?" Dad dropped his fork on his dinner plate with a loud clatter. "We'll be here forever at the rate you're eating."

Mom held up a finger as she swallowed. "Latest research says if you eat slowly, you'll feel full faster." Mom was always on the mission to lose weight. She had every diet book ever published. She also kept a stack of magazines, each of them advertising the latest fad diet. They were stacked on her bedside table, right next to her sleep mask.

"That's the most cockamamie thing I've ever heard." Dad tossed his napkin on his plate. "And I'm a doctor."

"Dr. Prepper." My sister took another swig from her can and hummed the jingle from the soda commercial. "Wouldn't you like to be a Prepper, too?"

"Very funny." Dad leaned back with his arms folded. "Is there anything else you'd like to tell me about the lights, Doomy?"

Dad sure knew how to suck the fun out of everything. "No sir."

"Are you sure?" Dad picked up a newspaper.

I stared at my plate. "Well, maybe one thing." I glanced up to see dad peering over the folded corner of his paper.

"What's that?"

"They turned green."

Dad lowered his paper into his lap. "Paula, how much water did you say you bottled?"

"Ten gallons per person." Mom held her breath as she stared into my dad's eyes. They seemed to be having a conversation in one single glance.

"We'll need three times that. Can you do it by tomorrow evening?"

Mom shook her head. "How could I possibly sterilize and bottle that much water in twenty-four hours, Kirk?"

"Good point." Dad took a deep breath and paused to look at my sister and then at me. "Get ready kids. We have a long night ahead."

KEEP YOUR NOSE CLEAN

KRISTY BRADSHAW (A.K.A. Kristy Kiss-up) was as predictable as a clock.

1. She always sat at the front of the room.
2. She got straight A's.
3. She had perfect attendance.

Kristy Bradshaw was absent from school today. Everyone said she had an orthodontist appointment, but I knew better.

"Peter," I whispered, trying not to draw attention to myself. "Psssst. Hey, Peter!"

"What, Doomy?"

"Kristy's absent."

Peter shrugged. "Who cares?"

"She's *never* absent."

"Maybe she got sick."

Wybie leaned across the aisle and cupped his mouth. "I heard she got braces."

"So why would she be out of school?"

"Besides the fact that they make everyone look like a brace face?" Wybie's curly red hair bounced as he laughed.

"I've heard they hurt," Peter said, opening his textbook.

"You know what I think?" I said, pulling the sleeve of Wybie's turtleneck so he could be close enough to hear my whisper.

Peter looked up from his book and leaned in, too.

"I think..." I paused dramatically, "...she was abducted by aliens."

Wybie snorted so hard a booger shot out of his nose and landed on his desk. "Aliens!"

"Shhh!"

But it was too late. Three classmates turned around. They were looking right at us.

"You mean Space Invaders," Peter said. "You know, the Atari game." He was quick on his feet. Always good at diversions.

"Atari's lame. Everyone knows Intellivision is better," one kid said. The others shrugged and returned to scribbling on their morning work.

"That was a close one," I said. "You know, Wybie, if you want to be part of this conversation, you're going to have to be a little more..."

"Discreet," Peter said.

"Yeah, dish-creet."

"No, not *dish*creet. *Dis*creet. It means being careful in your speech. You don't want to draw attention to us."

"Yeah, that."

"So why do you think she was abducted by aliens, Doomy?" Peter neatly wrote the answers to his morning work.

I peeked over at Peter's paper. He narrowed his eyes before covering his answers. "Because of the lights."

"What lights?" Wybie studied the booger still on his desk.

"The ones in the sky doo-doo head." I scribbled an answer on my paper.

Wybie got eye level with the booger, resting his nose on the desk. "Well, doo-doo head, they've always been there and haven't abducted anyone."

"*Yet.*" Peter chimed in without looking up from his paper.

I erased the answer I'd written. "And that was before they changed."

"Wait-a-stinking-minute." Wybie picked the booger off his desk and ate it. "So, you're telling me the lights are different?"

My stomach soured. "You're disgusting, you know that, don't you?" I turned to face Peter. "So, I think we need to make a plan. Maybe have a code word or something. That way if we're abducted, we can use the code word to send for help."

"And how do you propose we do that? You think we're going to be able to use the phone? My parents have a party line and the neighbors talk for hours."

"With these," I said, pulling two walkie-talkies out of my backpack.

Peter's glasses wobbled on his nose as he raised an eyebrow. "Where'd you get those?"

"Borrowed them from my dad's secret stash."

"Shouldn't you have asked?" Peter took the device. "They look military grade."

"I can neither confirm nor deny the existence of military grade walkie-talkies."

"Except I'm holding one," Peter said.

"Hey, I want one, too." Wybie had a finger up his nose.

"Later. And stop doing that."

Wybie shrugged.

"Turn in your morning work and line up for recess," Mrs. Nebula said, interrupting our super-important conversation. Wybie leapt out of his seat and grabbed his jacket from the coat rack. Thankfully, that meant he wasn't picking his nose for at least two seconds.

I turned in my blank page and Mrs. Nebula wagged her finger at me. "You'll have to stay inside during recess."

"No recess? Does that mean I get to help you grade papers? Oh, I know! I could test all the chalk on the chalkboard and make sure it doesn't make that awful screeching noise. You know how the class hates that. Or maybe I could just tell you about the time I—"

"On second thought," Mrs. Nebula said, staring right at me. I looked at the ground. Couldn't let her turn me to stone. Even if it was a good alternative to missing playground time. "Go on outside, Doomy."

I glanced up at her and squinted. That was easy! In fact, she changed her mind a little too quickly.

BE A TEAM PLAYER

RECESS PROMISED some of my favorite things.

1. Girl chases on the playground.
2. Army men battles with my friends.
3. Freedom from Mrs. Nebula who always stays inside.

"I'll be going outside today." Mrs. Nebula buttoned her coat.

My jaw dropped to the ground. *Great.* That explained why she changed her mind. She was coming out to spy on me!

Mrs. Nebula grinned as she held the door open. "Getting chilly, kids. Zip up."

"Ugh," I moaned as I marched past her.

"Where's Christopher?" Peter asked as he headed for a shady spot under the tree, his typical retreat for games. Christopher was in one of the other fifth grade classes but always joined us for army battles.

"How should I know? Where's Mrs. Stewart?" I glared at Mrs. Nebula's back. "How dare she come outside on a day like today?"

"Chill, Doomy." Peter dumped his little green men on the ground. "Mrs. Stewart is home sick. Someone had to take her place. Mrs. Nebula's the next choice."

"Do you really believe she's sick?"

"Sure." Peter shrugged. "Flu's been going around."

"Don't you think I would have heard about that?" I kicked the dirt. "My dad sees everyone in town at his practice. He would have mentioned it."

"Not everyone goes to the doctor for the flu, Doomy." Peter lined up his figurines in a neat row preparing them for battle.

"Or maybe she was abducted just like Kristy Bradshaw."

Peter let out a long sigh. "You've been watching too much Mork and Mindy."

"Doomy has a point though," Wybie said sitting cross-legged next to Peter. "Nicholas is out, too."

"Nicholas?" Peter looked up. It was like he realized something but didn't want to say it. He squinted like he was concentrating. "From Mr. Mercury's class?"

Wybie nodded.

"That's four," I said.

Peter rolled his eyes. "Big deal. Four people is hardly cause for conspiracy theories."

"Not conspiracy theories," I corrected. "Alien abductions."

"C'mon," Wybie said flicking a soldier on his side. He was a good flicker. Probably had lots of practice with his boogers. "You don't actually believe any of that, do you?"

"Then tell me why you don't see any girls chasing me today."

Peter and Wybie both stopped what they were doing and looked up. They glanced at the playground. It was a wasteland. It wasn't just Christopher, Kristy, Mrs. Stewart, and Nicholas who were missing. It was a lot more than that. About half of the fifth grade was gone.

"Like I said." Peter swallowed hard. "It's the flu."

"If you say so. But I'm going to start an investigation. Not taking any chances. You can join me if you want."

"I will!" Wybie's hand shot into the air. "We can call ourselves the Three Musketeers."

"That's lame. And not at all discreet." Peter lined up another row of army men. "Look out, Doomy. Garcia's behind you."

I turned to see Bryce Garcia strolling toward me. "Ugh," I moaned.

Bryce stood ten feet tall, no joke, and looked like a moose in a field of deer. "More like the Three Stooges," Bryce said with a laugh. He had on a baseball t-shirt that was three sizes too small. It showed off his muscles. No one had muscles like that in fifth grade. It just wasn't normal.

"Go away. We're talking." I crossed my arms. Bryce once told us his cousin was in the band Menudo. He said he could get autographs. All the girls went gah gah over him. Including Melissa Bennettt. Wybie and Bryce may have been best friends, but I didn't like that he was always butting in. Plus, the muscle thing. Not like I was jealous.

"I have some information you might find interesting." Bryce handed me a paper.

"What's this?" I grabbed it and read the words typed across the top of the page. "Area 51: Experiment 362."

Peter glanced at the paper. "Where'd you find that?"

"My dad worked in the lab." Bryce grabbed the report back.

"Isn't that all the way in Arizona?" I folded my arms again.

"Nevada," Peter said.

I rolled my eyes. "Same difference."

"When I was on my way home yesterday, I saw the lights change." Bryce shoved a hand in his pocket and leaned against the tree, while still waving the paper in the other hand.

Bryce was trying to pull a fast one, but I wasn't falling for it. "You did?" I narrowed my eyes. "What did it look like?"

"Seemed like a signal, if you ask me." Bryce shrugged. "So, I did some snooping in my dad's office.

Swiped the report right off his desk. You can have it—"

"Great." I reached to take it, but Bryce pulled away and held the paper over his head. He was about as tall as Bigfoot, so I had to jump to get it. Every time I got close, he just lifted it higher.

"On one condition." Bryce waved the paper.

My patience were wearing thin. "And what's that?"

"You let me join your little club."

"Forget it, Bryce. It's just the three of us. Me, Peter, and Wybie."

"He has valuable information," Peter whispered.

"You're making a mistake." Bryce shook his head. He lifted the paper eye level and made a motion like he was going to tear it to pieces.

I stared him down. "Fine. But only because we need your report."

"Smart man," Bryce said. He folded the paper and tucked it into his back pocket.

Peter pushed his glasses into place and wiggled his nose. "Cuatro."

"What?" I sat next to him.

"Cuatro. It's Spanish for four." Bryce squatted next to Wybie.

Peter was busy assembling his men into three lines. "Might be a good name for our team but we can make it an acronym instead."

I put three men in a triangle formation. "An acronym?"

"It's like when each letter stands for a word." Peter looked up over the rim of his glasses.

"Quatro...Quit Underwear And Try..." Wybie said, thinking aloud.

"Cuatro starts with a 'c' not a 'q'," Peter said with a sigh. "Try four instead."

"Four...Finding Our Underwear Ripped." Wybie made fart noises as he knocked over some of my army men. There were rules to our game, but they only made sense to us.

"Curses!" I said, moving my men to the side. I'd been too distracted. Melissa Bennett abandoned her failed box ball game and marched up behind Wybie. I'd seen her bossing the other kids around. They'd had an argument and ran off to climb the monkey bars. Not that I was watching her or anything because that would be weird.

"That's the stupidest thing I ever heard." She stood there with her hands on her hips.

"Eavesdrop much?" I said. My cheeks felt hot and I quickly looked away. Why'd I always feel like I was going to vomit whenever I talked to her? Ugh!

"All the time," Melissa said. "Just so you know." She held Bryce's document, reading it. "This was very controversial."

"Wait..." Bryce stammered as he turned around like a dog chasing his tail. "How'd you..."

"Never mind," Melissa said with a smirk. "You should also know," she put a hand on her waist and popped her hip, "it's Friends Investigate Various

Events." Her short brown curls bounced on her shoulders as she shifted side to side.

"That spells five, Melissa. Not four." Peter stood up and pushed his glasses in place.

I leapt to my feet. "Yeah, there's only four of us. Me, Wybie, Peter, and..." I paused to look at our fourth member. Mr. Macho Menudo. Mr. Tough Guy. Mr. All-the-girls-love-me. My throat ached. We couldn't exclude him. Not when he was Wybie's best friend. And especially not when he had such interesting information. "And Bryce."

"Five," Melissa said with a grin.

"Can't you count?" Wybie scrambled to his feet.

His shoe crunched a plastic soldier and he tried to hide it by dragging it under his foot.

"As a matter of fact, I can." Melissa put her hand out and Peter, with a knowing smile, shook it. "I'm including myself on your team. My dad was acting funny yesterday. He listened to his telegraph all night. Stared at it like he was watching an episode of Cagney and Lacey."

"Telegraph?" Wybie laughed and a booger shot out of his nose.

"Yes, telegraph." She glanced at Wybie, then at the glob of snot on the ground. "Anyway, I can see that you're going to need me." She reached out to shake my hand. This wasn't what I'd bargained for. "That makes five. You're welcome. Now, let's get started."

DO NOT IGNORE CLUES

THE SCHOOL BELL signals three of my favorite things.

1. Lunch.
2. Recess.
3. Dismissal.

"Not so fast," Mrs. Nebula said as I zipped up my coat and threw my bag over my shoulder. "Where do you think you're going?" She grabbed my arm.

"Home," I said. I tried to shrug her off, but her grip was too strong. I needed to meet up with the F.I.V.E.'s so we could make plans. We'd spent the rest of recess discussing the missing students and we agreed to meet after school. We were going to investigate this together and get to the bottom of these strange disappearances.

"Oh no you're not. It's detention for you." Mrs. Nebula picked up an abandoned teddy bear off the floor and held it in the crook of her arm. "Where'd this come from?" Mrs. Nebula whispered to herself with a sigh.

"Detention? For what?"

She seemed to stare off into space for a moment. "What was I saying?" She blinked and rubbed her face. "Oh yes. Do I need to remind you of that test grade?"

Not the test again! Distraction was the only way out of this. "You're looking very nice today, Mrs. Nebula. That extra layer of Aqua Net really held your hair in place."

Mrs. Nebula paled a bit. "My hair?"

"Yeah, and..." There had to be something else I could compliment but as I glanced at her I realized she didn't look so good at all. Not only was she pale, but even her mole looked lifeless. The hairs on it fell limp against her cheek. "You okay, Mrs. Nebula? You're looking a little sick."

Her eyes glossed over. She clenched the teddy bear tighter and stared off into space. "Go to the office, Doomy."

Shrugging, I headed toward the classroom door, my freedom just a few steps away.

"Oh, and Doomy?"

Drat! I was doomed. "Yes, Mrs. Nebula?" I waited for her response and when none came, I glanced back over my shoulder. My eyes must have been playing tricks on me because she was nowhere in sight. "Mrs. Nebula?"

Something felt wrong.

Very, very wrong.

"Mrs. Nebula? Where'd you go?" At the back of the room is a door. It's a supply closet that holds our half-finished projects and extra boxes of markers. She must have gone inside there. I crept toward it. "Mrs. Nebula? Are you in there?" I opened the door and peeked into the closet, but she wasn't inside. "Huh," I said with a shrug. *She disappeared. Just like that.* "So strange."

"What's strange?" Peter's voice made me jump. I thought he'd gotten on the bus.

"She's gone," I said to Peter who stood in the classroom doorway.

Peter didn't seem to hear me because he continued talking. "And why the heck are you still here?"

"Well, I didn't want to be but Mrs. Nebula—"

"Went home," Peter said as he shoved something in his backpack.

"But she was just here," I said.

"Well, she must have slipped out the door when you weren't looking."

"Did you see her?" My throat felt tight.

"No, but if she's not in the classroom then where else would she be?"

"Abducted. Just like the rest of them."

Peter laughed.

"What else would it be? She was standing right here a minute ago. We were talking—"

"Stop wigging out, Doomy." Peter walked toward the wall of windows lining the far wall of our classroom. He squinted as he looked through his thick lenses. "Looks like it's going to storm. You should probably go home. Don't want to get caught in the rain."

"Aren't you going to miss the bus?" My backpack weighed my shoulder down, so I slipped the other strap in place. With the bag secured on my back, I headed for the door.

"Good point." Peter grabbed his bag and a paper fluttered to the floor.

"You think the F.I.V.E.'s will still meet tonight?" I asked.

"Not in this storm," Peter said.

I shrugged. "You're probably right." The sound of bus engines roared to life.

Peter's eyes grew wide. "Let's go!"

We raced out of the classroom, past Principal Geller's office, and straight through the front doors of the building.

Engines rumbled as the buses waited for stragglers to board. My bike, which had been secured on the rack, sprung to life as I rolled it on the pavement.

"I'll call you later," Peter shouted from his open window. He stuck his arm out and waved but I heard the bus driver yell at him, and he promptly tucked his arm back inside. He disappeared a second as he ducked behind the tall bus seat. He reappeared a moment later holding the walkie-talkie. "Channel 10."

"Got it!" I swung a leg over the seat of my bike.

"We can fill in the F.I.V.E.'s another time," I started to say but his bus lurched into gear. Gravel kicked up under the tires as it rolled out of the loop. The bus rounded the turn before pulling out onto the road. Movement above the roof caught my eye. A small blip of something shiny whirled in the sky.

"Peter!" A silver crescent slipped out from behind a cloud. It was the same thing I'd seen the other day. "Look!" I shouted while pointing toward the sky. The noise from the engines drowned out my voice as another bus pulled into the loop. Peter's bus gained speed, and he waved out the back window. I pointed at the sky, but Peter didn't see me because he had already returned to his seat.

The silver crescent snuck back behind a cloud. The lights flashed pink. Then green.

The teachers stood in the bus loop making sure

the kids boarded safely. They didn't seem to notice this strange phenomenon. Neither did any of the safety patrols. Or the kids walking in groups. Or the ones on their bikes.

"Don't you see it?" I shouted. But no one heard me.

Wybie was up ahead on his skateboard, riding alongside Bryce who was on his bike. The reflectors on Bryce's spokes caught the colored lights in the sky.

I pedaled to catch up to them. A dirt-caked teddy bear lay on the ground and I started to steer around it. But then I thought to get a closer look. My foot slipped off the pedal as I tried to break. The bear looked so familiar. Almost like the one Mrs. Nebula was holding. As I reached down to pick it up, a car horn blared. I jumped. Principal Geller sat in the driver's seat of his new sedan. He gave me a serious look, which meant I better move out of his way.

Wybie and Bryce were nearly out of sight. "Hey," I called. "Wait up!"

My feet scrambled onto the pedals as I sped away, leaving the dirt-caked teddy bear lying in the middle of the dusty road.

ALWAYS KEEP A SUPPLY OF TOILET PAPER

MY MOM HAD BEEN PREPPING for years. She'd accumulated lots of stuff.

1. Enough food to feed an army.
2. Things to keep us from getting bored, like magazines and card games.
3. Toilet paper.

I stared at the stack of newspapers sitting by the front door. "What's that for?" I asked, still breathless from my bike ride.

"You never know when you're going to need it, Doomy. You could have to poop and there'd be nothing to—"

"Mom. Stop. Just don't." I grabbed the milk from the fridge and took a swig from the carton.

"Don't be disgusting, Doomy." Mom handed me a glass.

I rolled my eyes. As if she hadn't just been talking about poop.

"All the kids at school today?" Mom asked as she sat at the table with a bowl of freshly washed grapes. Her voice had concern in it, but her face said this was as normal as using newspaper for toilet paper.

"No." I shook my head. "Kristy Bradshaw was absent. And a bunch of other kids, too."

"The PTA secretary didn't show up for our meeting." Mom breathed the words like she was afraid to say them out loud. "Can you believe that? I had to jot the minutes on a napkin!"

I snatched some of the grapes from the bowl and popped them into my mouth. "Peter says it's the flu."

"Who has the flu?" Dad adjusted his pants as he walked into the room.

"Lots of kids." I poured a glass of milk and drank it. "Like half my class."

"You don't say." Dad pulled out a chair. He straddled the seat before sitting. "Are you sure it's the flu?

My office has been quiet all week. In fact, my receptionist never showed today."

"Didn't show for work?" Mom made a weird huffing sound as she leaned back. "Maybe she needs to find a new job."

"Don't be irrational, Paula."

"Speaking of not being irrational," my sister said as she walked into the room in a neon pink leotard. Her hair was in a high pony and she had sweatbands on each wrist. "You're both the most rational people I have ever met. That's why you're *not* going to object when I leave the house at six for the dance off."

Dad's brow furrowed. My dad had eyebrows that could rival the guy on Magnum P.I. so the giant hairballs nearly swallowed his eyes.

"Oh, by the way, can I borrow the car?" Gabrielle chomped on her gum before blowing a bubble. It popped and some of it got into her big bangs.

"Borrow the car? You don't even have a license!" The chair screeched as mom stood up suddenly.

"Alright, then you gotta drive me." Gabby dangled the keys from her fingertips.

Mom raised an eyebrow. "Not when you ask like that."

"Please?" Gabby placed the keys on the counter.

"You know I don't approve of all this dancing." Mom swiped the keys. "It isn't natural."

"But mom, it's like the biggest contest of the season. And since a lot of the girls in my class were out sick—"

"Out sick?" Dad scratched his forehead. His giant mustache nearly hid his frown.

Gabrielle nodded. "With them too sick to compete—"

"There's no competition." I said it for her.

"That's not what I was going to say, dweeb."

"It's what you were thinking. Besides, you haven't had a single lesson." I grabbed a bag of chips from the pantry and popped it open. "Watching MTV doesn't count."

"Shut up, Doomy." Blabby Gabby marched out of the room, her sneakers squeaking on the linoleum.

"Not so fast," Dad called after her.

Gabby stopped and turned around. "Ugh, what?"

"Doomy." Dad cleared his throat. "Can you tell us more about what you saw yesterday?"

"It wasn't just yesterday. Happened again today."

Mom's jaw went slack. Dad put a hand on his hip and another on his chin. My sister blew bubbles with her gum. I stared at them all.

"Bryce says he saw it, too." I thought about mentioning the report from Area 51 but decided against it. My dad would likely resort to drastic measures and I didn't need that in my life right now. "Melissa said her dad listened to his telegraph click for hours."

"Telegraph?" Dad coughed. "That adds a layer to the cake, doesn't it? I don't think we have a choice. It's time to commence with Operation FOIL." He went to the kitchen sink and filled a glass with cold water.

You'd think that FOIL stood for a funny bunch of words. Peter called that an acronym. Something cool like Fat Octopus Is Lying. Or First, Outer, Inner, Last—that's a tool my sister uses to help her remember the rules in Algebra. She says it is an order of operation though I'm not sure how that helps. FOIL, however, didn't stand for either one of those things. Oh no, it sure didn't. In fact, it wasn't even an acronym.

Operation FOIL was the reason for our stockpile of aluminum foil. It also meant I'd be too busy to radio Peter.

Dad downed his drink, wiped his mouth with is sleeve, and placed the empty glass on the counter. "We have thirty minutes."

"But I'm going to miss the dance off!" My sister threw her arms up and made a face at me. "Nice going, Doomy."

"How's this *my* fault?"

"Everyone knows you make up stories for attention." Gabby's face grew red.

How dare she make such an accusation! This meant war. "Oh yeah? Well at least I don't wear a stupid letterman jacket like your bo-oo-ooy-friend."

"Is that supposed to be an insult, dork? Because I can assure you, Doomy, that my boyfriend is a thousand times cooler than you."

"Boyfriend?" Dad choked.

"It's nothing to be concerned about, Kirk." Mom patted his back. "You know how kids are. Just a silly crush."

"It's not silly!" My sister folded her arms. "And it's not a crush!"

I smirked. "Yeah, it's her bo-oo-ooy-friend."

"I'm going to get you, you little twerp!" Gabby charged, tripping on the threshold between the kitchen and dining room.

"You can't catch me!" I bolted out of the room and looped around the couch. When I reached the kitchen again, I stopped at my mom's side and hid behind her.

"Can too!"

"Can—!"

"Alright, that's enough." Mom stood at the sink, rinsed the bubbly suds off a plate like this was completely normal (it was) and continued washing the dishes. "We need to work together."

"Fine. But I'm not going to like it." Gabby pulled a sweater over her leotard.

"No one said you had to." Dad handed Gabby a roll of aluminum foil. "You just have to do it."

Mom dried her hands. She pulled a second roll of aluminum foil out of the drawer. "Time to wrap the house."

NEVER FOIL WITH ALUMINUM FOIL

NEIGHBORS CAN BE PROBLEMATIC.

1. They bring free food. It's always tuna casserole.
2. They pop in for a visit when your homerun shatters their living room window.
3. They make mountains out of molehills.

My neighbor grumbled. "Morning, Doomy." Mr. Kranker (or Mr. Kranker McKrankyPants as I liked to call him) pulled his bathrobe tighter as he shuffled toward his garbage bins at the curb. "Your family kept the neighborhood up half the night with their shenanigans."

I shrugged. I wasn't the boss of the family. My dad was. Like I was supposed to stop him? Aluminum foil was the only way to protect us from the mind-reading aliens. "I gotta go, Mr. Kranker."

"Heading to school?"

"Yeah." It was a weekday. I didn't think this needed explaining.

He shielded his eyes from the sunlight reflecting off the surface of my freshly-wrapped house. "That's a lot of foil you got there."

That was stating the obvious. "I guess so," I said, turning back and staring up at the giant silver box. The house once looked normal, like all the others on the street. Now it was an embarrassment.

Mr. Kranker narrowed his eyes. Puckered his lips. "Alien invasion, huh?" He laughed. He laughed so hard he coughed.

The sunlight bounced off the house straight into my eyes, making them water like a faucet. "You could say that," I said as I wiped away the tears.

"Maybe you ought to try shrink wrap."

"Very funny," I mumbled under my breath as I threw my backpack over my shoulder. The bag was heavier than usual since I'd packed an extra bottle of Yoo-hoo with my fluffernutter sandwich.

"Maybe I ought to protect my home, too. You know, since aluminum foil prevents radiation and mind reading."

"I don't think your brain needs protecting," I said.

"Why's that, Doomy?"

Probably because he didn't have one. "Just a hunch."

Mr. Kranker pulled a hankie from his bathrobe pocket and blew his nose into it. He mumbled something before dragging the trashcan to his garage.

Shaking my head, I hopped on my bike and zipped past a few houses. At the stop sign, I paused. Up on the hill, Mrs. Blackwood stood on her front porch wearing floral pajamas. Curlers hung from her hair. She clutched onto a teddy bear with a far-off look in her eyes.

"Feeling alright, Mrs. Blackwood?"

She nodded. "Just fine, Doomy."

She didn't sound fine. "Peter says the flu's been going around. Maybe you ought to go see my dad."

"Good idea. Thank you, Doomy." She never smiled. She just kept staring straight past me.

Overhead, the sky darkened like it does before a storm. The sound of thunder never followed. And neither did the rain. I tilted my head back and looked up into the clouds. They were pink, just like the lights were when they changed. The clouds flickered like lightning and then turned green.

"Did you see that?" I asked, still staring up at the sky. Mrs. Blackwood didn't respond. The sky flashed again. "That! That right there!" I pointed at the clouds and turned toward my neighbor. She wasn't on her porch anymore. I scanned the yard, but she was gone! "Mrs. Blackwood? Where'd you go?" I leapt off my bike, letting it clatter to the ground, and raced up her driveway. She was nowhere in sight. She'd just completely vanished into thin air. The only evidence that she'd ever been there was a single fuzzy pink slipper stuck in the mud by her flowerbeds. "Whoa," I whispered. "She vanished just like Mrs. Nebula, Kristy, and everyone else."

As I turned to jump back on my bike, Peter's school bus idled at the stop sign. It proceeded through the intersection and then zoomed past. I pedaled as fast as I could, trying to catch up. The cloud-filled sky flashed between pink and green, strobing like a David Bowie concert. When I rounded the corner into the school parking lot, the lights bounced off the roofs of the buses. They reflected off the windows of the school, too. Surely, someone else saw it. Anyone.

Wybie zipped past on his skateboard. He did an ollie over the curb, flipped the tip of the board with his toe, and swiped it under his arm like a pro. He headed for the entrance, dodging classmates and zig zagging around the first graders.

"Wybie," I called. "Hey, Wybie!" He slipped into the school as I tried to park my bike. It clattered to the ground, but I left it there as I rushed to catch up. Something was wrong with him. Maybe this wasn't Wybie at all. Maybe it was someone pretending to be him. This was a real-life version of Invasion of the Body Snatchers! I raced up behind him and tapped him on the shoulder. "Wybie!"

He removed his headphones. "Hey, Doomy. What's up?"

"Uh...uh...I just..." It *was* Wybie after all. Now I

needed to come up with an excuse for my behavior. "I just wondered what you were listening to."

"Nothing." He shoved his Walkman into his backpack, but I saw the name on the cassette.

"Menudo? Really? You can't honestly like that."

"What's wrong with it?" Wybie shrugged.

We rounded the corner and reached our classroom. When we entered, I saw each one of my classmates (the ones who weren't absent) seated at their desks. They all had cone-shaped hats made from aluminum foil on their heads.

"If you can't wrap your house, you gotta wrap your head," a couple of kids said in unison.

"Very funny, guys." I hung up my backpack, then

took off my coat and slipped into my seat. Little did they know I had a layer of foil on my head under my baseball cap. But I wasn't about to tell them that my dad insisted I wear it. Or that I felt safer with it on.

Peter was the only one without a hat and he looked concerned. "You okay, Doomy? You never radioed last night"

"As you can see," I pointed at my classmates, "my dad had us prepare for the apocalypse." I pulled a pencil from my desk. "Saw something weird on my way here."

"I saw it, too." Peter put his pencil to his paper and started his morning work. "Mrs. Blackwood disappeared."

"Just like Mrs. Nebula did yesterday." My eyes widened as I realized my dad wasn't overreacting. And that people were finally believing me. I wasn't a conspiracy theorist! I swear.

"Mrs. Nebula didn't disappear," Peter said calmly. He kept his head down, engaged in his work, as he wagged his pencil at the front of the room where our teacher stood dragging chalk against the chalkboard.

"Are you sure about that?" Wybie pointed as the teacher dusted her hands and turned around. But it wasn't Mrs. Nebula. Nope. This woman had a sharp nose, beady eyes, and pointed eyebrows which made her look mean, and cranky, and not at all nice.

I gasped. My worst fear was confirmed. "A substitute."

TRY TO TRICK YOUR SUBSTITUTE

SUBSTITUTE TEACHERS CAN HAVE good qualities.

1. You can get away with stuff you wouldn't normally do.
2. They can't turn you into stone.
3. They don't know your name.

"Doomy Prepper," the substitute said as she stared straight at me while taking attendance.

"It's Peter Peterson," I said with a smirk.

She narrowed her eyes. "Doomy Prepper."

"What?" I stared back.

"My name is Ms. Martian," she said, "and usually the proper response is 'here' or 'present.'"

"Ugh," I groaned as I looked at Peter. "How'd she know my name?"

"Duh. She has an attendance list."

"Yeah, but it's not like they come with photos of us and she's looking right at me."

"Everyone knows you're Dr. Prepper's kid. C'mon, Doomy. Don't look so surprised."

I slumped back in my seat. "But I've never seen her before."

"Me either, but so what?"

"So what? SO WHAT?" My head felt like it might explode.

Peter's jaw went slack as he pushed his glasses back.

"Neither one of us has ever seen her before, she knows me by name, and our real teacher is missing. I'd say that's a pretty big 'so what,' don't you?"

"Perhaps." Peter reclined in his seat as he put his pencil down. He'd completed his morning work in record time.

I slammed my pencil on my desk. Peter jumped. Three kids in front of me turned around and the substitute's lips pursed so tight it looked like she'd sucked on a lemon.

"Keep your cool," Peter said, shoving his pencil inside his desk.

"Is there a problem, Doomy?" The substitute crossed her arms.

I sunk in my seat. "No, ma'am."

"Good." Ms. Martian squinted as she scanned the classroom. "Now, children, I want you all to remove those ridiculous foil hats."

The class groaned but followed instructions anyway. Bryce and Wybie each shoved their hats inside their desks. Melissa delivered hers to the coat rack. Peter just stared at me wide-eyed.

I wasn't about to remove my baseball cap. No one could know I really had foil on my head. Or that I wanted it there for my protection.

"Good. Now that that's taken care of," Ms. Martian said as the heels of her granny shoes clicked on the floor, "we can get started."

"But where's Mrs. Nebula?" Wybie's hand shot into the air as he asked the question. Technically, he only raised his hand so he couldn't be yelled at, but he still hadn't waited to be called on.

"She's out sick." Ms. Martian turned her back to us as she rummaged around in her bag. She pulled out a roll of candy and popped one into her mouth.

"Is it the flu?" Peter asked. His voice was hushed and my skin prickled. We exchanged a knowing look. "Seems everyone's got it. Well, everyone except us."

The substitute teacher whirled around. "Not yet."

"What a way to be positive," Melissa said. She smeared gloss on her lips and smacked them together. When she caught me staring, she smiled. My cheeks betrayed me and flushed red hot.

"Aren't we a feisty one?" Ms. Martian paced up and down the rows between our desks before returning to the front of the room.

Melissa smirked. "You could say that." She winked at me like she was trying to say something, but I just sat there like a dummy.

"I'm keeping my eye on you." Ms. Martian pointed at Melissa who groaned.

"Will we be doing our lessons today?" Peter thumbed through his textbook. "We left off on page seventy-one. I'd be happy to present a review."

"That won't be necessary." Ms. Martian had a strange smile on her face. "I have something much better planned."

"Yes!" Wybie cheered. "Is it recess?"

"No." Ms. Martian raised an eyebrow. "We're going on a field trip."

SECURE PERMISSION SLIPS FOR SURVIVAL

FIELD TRIPS ARE a great addition to our educational experience.

1. We're not in the classroom.
2. We can goof off on the bus.
3. The cool moms bring candy.

"My mom didn't pack any candy," I said after Ms. Martian made the announcement of this unexpected trip. "She's the room mom so she always comes with us."

Peter shot his hand into the air. "My parents never signed a permission slip," he said without waiting to be called on. "What about the fee? And our lunch? And—"

"Peter!" Ms. Martian clicked her heels and straightened her posture. "Peter Peterson, is it?"

A lump the size of a fireball candy formed in his throat. Peter swallowed hard and the lump stuck there as he nodded.

"Ah, well, I see then." The substitute turned to her desk and pulled a paper off a stack. She tapped a pencil to it, scribbled something, then returned it with the others. "Now, everyone, grab your coats. Pish posh!"

"Where are we going?" I asked.

"You'll find out soon enough." Ms. Martian smirked.

Peter and I exchanged looks. He tipped his head. "Go on, Doomy," he whispered.

We were definitely thinking the same thing. We needed to bug her with loads of questions. "Should we bring our lunches?"

"I don't think that's necessary," Ms. Martian said.

Bryce popped open a bag of barbeque flavored chips and started eating them two at a time. "But I'll starve."

"You won't starve." Wybie nudged him with his elbow.

Bryce's stomach growled as he shoved another handful of chips in his mouth. Crumbs fell to the floor.

"Fine. Bring your lunches." Ms. Martian slipped her purse over her shoulder. Then she picked up a green and black striped bag off the floor. "You might want to bring your coat, too."

"How about hats?" I squinted at Peter who, again, seemed to understand.

"What about mittens and scarves?" Peter covered his mouth as he snickered.

I kept my cool. "Do you think it'll be cold where we're going?"

"Yes. It'll definitely be cold where you're going." Ms. Martian's eyes flickered. "Bring whatever you want. Just collect your things and get on the bus."

Melissa eyed me as she went to the coat rack. She grabbed her backpack, which had a rainbow kitten pattern on it, and started for the door.

"Wait up," I mouthed. She nodded. I quickly shoved some stuff from my desk into my backpack and threw it over my shoulder.

Peter eyed me as he swiped his bag and joined us at the door. "Where do you think we're going?"

"Got me," Wybie said as he came up behind us, eating a gummy bear.

"It's not even lunch and you're eating candy?" Peter watched in disgust as Wybie chewed the bear. It stuck to his teeth in neon shades of orange and green.

Wybie picked the candy from a front tooth. "What's it to you?"

"Nothing." Peter shrugged.

"Can we go now?" I sighed.

Bryce finished his bag of chips and wiped his stained fingers on his jeans. "Yeah. What are we waiting for?"

We shuffled past Principal Geller's office. He sat at his desk shoving fistfuls of candy into his mouth.

"See you later, Principal Geller," I said with a wave. He didn't respond. Just stared past me like I wasn't even there. "Principal Geller?" I poked my head into his office and saw a teddy bear on his desk. He picked it up and held it in the crook of his arm. It was the same bear I'd seen Mrs. Nebula holding. I gasped. "Oh no!"

I stared a minute longer watching Principal Geller hug the teddy bear and shove more candy in his mouth. He suddenly made eye contact with me and I bee-lined it out the door. The air had turned cold and it snapped at my face. Gray clouds crowded out the colorful lights in the sky.

When I caught up to Peter, he was standing with Wybie looking up at the sky. Melissa and Bryce were already in line to get on the bus and we dashed over to them.

"Did you notice the principal?" I clenched onto the straps of my backpack waiting for a response but the F.I.V.E.'s were working their way onto the bus. "Does anyone else feel like something's off?"

"Other than we never had permission slips?" Peter zipped his coat.

Melissa turned around. "Or that there was never an announcement?"

I nodded. "Yeah, that."

"Nah," Wybie said a little too loud. "I remember something about it."

I snapped my head up. "You do?"

"No, he doesn't," Peter said. "Wybie can't even remember his homework assignments."

"Do, too!" Wybie pegged Peter in the forehead with a gummy.

Peter immediately rubbed the spot. "Knock it off, dweeb."

"Boys!" Ms. Martian clapped her hands. "Behave." She gave us each a stern look then climbed on the bus and claimed the seat directly behind the driver.

For a fleeting second, I actually missed Mrs. Nebula.

We stepped on board next.

"Hi Mr. Wooster," I said to the bus driver, recognizing him as my neighbor two houses down.

He nodded as he stared out the windshield. "Nice day for a drive, Doomy."

"Where are we going, anyway?" It was a simple question. Peter had a point about the permission slips. And everything else, too. It was high time we knew where this field trip was headed. Unblinking, Mr. Wooster, ignored me.

"The zoo," Ms. Martian said. "We're going to the zoo."

If I'd known that's what the field trip was, I never would have gotten on the bus.

DISCOVER YOUR CODE WORDS

THE F.I.V.E.'S were great about three things.

1. We worked together.
2. We spied trouble.
3. We never overlooked the obvious.

A sign for the zoo pointed right. The bus took a sharp turn left. "I love the zoo!" Wybie cheered.

Peter glared at him and thumbed over his shoulder. "Except everyone knows it's the other direction."

"It is?" Wybie sat up and turned abruptly to look out the back window.

"Yup." I gulped. "We're going the wrong way." My suspicions were right all along. I should have never got on this bus! I quickly gestured for Peter and the rest of the F.I.V.E.'s to come closer.

Bryce and Melissa quietly snuck out of their seats. They squeezed into the row with us.

"What's going on?" Bryce asked as he pulled a bologna sandwich from his bag.

"I'm not sure," Peter said. "But we're definitely not going to the zoo. And I don't think this is any monkey business."

"What makes you say that?" Bryce took a bite of his sandwich.

"Our classmates are missing. Our teacher vanished. And now we're headed on a one-way trip to an unknown destination." I counted the items on my fingers. "That's three. What more do you want?"

Bryce shrugged. "I'd like a Devil Dog."

"I'm not talking about food you dimwit." I sighed loudly. "I'm talking about this surprise trip. The one our parents don't know about. How much longer are we going to let this continue before we do anything about it? We've got a put a stop to whatever this is."

"Good point," Wybie said. "Do you still have the walkie-talkies?"

"I've got the one Doomy gave me yesterday." Peter reached in his bag and pulled out the device. "What good will that do?"

"My dad turned his on last night." I grabbed the walkie from Peter. "Maybe I can radio him and ask him to send help."

"But you'd have to know what channel he's on." Peter pointed to the dial.

I slumped in my seat. "Good point."

"My mom and I have a code word," Melissa whispered. "For things..."

"What kind of things?" Bryce licked mustard off his fingers.

"Things boys wouldn't understand. So, let's just say we use a code, okay?" Melissa took the walkie from me. "Maybe your family has one, too."

Now that would make sense. We'd prepared everything for the end of the world. Everything except a code word. Guess my parents never expected us to be separated in the event of an apocalypse. It was the only thing we hadn't prepared for.

"I don't think so." I shook my head. As I did, a thought came to mind. Maybe there *was* a code word. And it was so coded I didn't even know it was a code until I had to figure out that it was a code. In that instant, I knew just how genius my dad really was. "Foil."

"What's foil?" Peter asked. His glasses slipped to the tip of his nose and he promptly pushed them back.

"It's what they did to their house," Wybie said trying not to laugh.

"Exactly." I pinched my lips tight.

"Okay, great we have a word." Melissa looked at the walkie. "But that doesn't help us figure out which channel to use."

"But it does," I said as I took the walkie back.

Bryce, having devoured his entire sandwich, belched. "How so?"

"Because it's not the only one." My hands shook

as I turned the dial. It clicked loudly with each twist. Ten, nine, eight. "Don't you see?"

"Not really," Bryce said grabbing for an apple. Peter snatched it away from him and stuck it in his backpack. "Hey, give that back."

"Later. Now be quiet." Peter didn't normally boss anyone around and I suddenly felt incredibly proud of him.

"FAST," I said, recalling another operation my dad had created. That was the one where we'd have to jump in the car and drive toward the mountains. We had a cabin there where we could survive for a super long time. I turned the dial three more clicks. Seven, six, five.

"Slow is more like it. Hurry it up," Wybie said as he blew his nose into a tissue.

"Shhhh." Peter put a finger to his lips. "Don't distract him."

"Go on, Doomy." Melissa tapped the walkie. Our eyes made contact and I smiled. I was going to save the day. I'd radio my dad and he'd call for help and we'd all be rescued.

"FREE." It was the third code. But it didn't really mean what people thought. It was instruction to lock ourselves in the storm shelter located in our basement. The only freedom we'd have was from zombies.

"What do these words have to do with anything?" Bryce asked.

"Shhhh," Peter said. "Go on, Doomy."

Wybie examined the contents of his tissue before tossing it on the floor. "Foil, fast, and free. That's three."

"Three words that all start with the letter f," I said.

"Big deal." Wybie shrugged.

"They all have the same amount of letters." I clicked the dial one more time. "Four."

MAKE YOUR DISCOVERIES IN SILENCE

WE LEARNED important things about Ms. Martian.

1. She was sneaky and clever.
2. She could eavesdrop on a conversation all the way from the front of the bus.
3. She respected our personal belongings.

"I'll take that," she said, holding her hand out for the walkie-talkie.

FOIL, FAST, and FREE. I stared at Peter in both awe and fear. We couldn't let her take it. I'd just discovered my dad's final code word: FOUR, which was also the channel he'd use for our communications. The problem was I didn't do it fast enough. Ms. Martian wanted my walkie, and I had a bad feeling something even worse would happen if I didn't give it to her.

Ms. Martian's open palm looked like a wrinkled pancake. "There will be no more nonsense on this bus ride."

"But..." I started to interject with my objection, but she wasn't having any of it.

"Hand it over. Now!" Ms. Martian's voice came as a sharp trill as she wiggled her fingers. "I haven't got all day."

Melissa flinched. She glanced at me, then at the walkie in my hand. "Go on, Doomy," Melissa whispered. "Give it to her." She wasn't one to give up so easily. Although I'd never tell her, I kind of admired her for it. Which made it seem strange she'd encourage me to surrender the one thing that might be our only form of communication and potential rescue.

Disappointed and defeated, I dropped the device into Ms. Martian's palm. What was I going to do now?

"That's a good boy." Ms. Martian patted my head before returning to her seat.

Wybie chucked a gummy at her head but missed and it tapped her shoulder.

Ms. Martian whipped around and glared at him. If I wasn't mistaken, I swear her eyes turned into little black slits.

"Did you see that?" I whispered.

Peter gulped. "I think I did."

The bus suddenly took a sharp turn and Wybie flew out of his seat. "Ugh," he said as he landed on me with a thud.

The impact hit me so hard I slid across the bench, smooshing Peter against the window.

Wybie's booger nose poked my eyeball and his hot, gummy bear breath blew directly up my nostril. "Dude, Doomy. You've got to lay off the hair gel. It's stuck to your scalp."

It's a good thing he didn't realize it wasn't hair product. I'd be embarrassed if he knew it was really aluminum foil. "And you've gotta lay off the candy," I replied. "I bet you have a dozen cavities."

"Just two," Wybie said, sitting up.

I secured my cap into place. "Is that all?"

Wybie shrugged.

"Can't breathe," Peter said, using the window to brace himself as he pushed me away.

"Sorry. Not like I planned that." I sat up and noticed Melissa staring at me. Well, not at *me*. At my head. She gestured to her forehead and I quickly put my hand to my own. A piece of foil stuck out from under my cap and my cheeks grew hot. I pulled the brim down, hiding my eyes in embarrassment.

Melissa shrugged, turned, and pressed her knees into the seat in front of her. She put her head back and closed her eyes like nothing ever happened.

Peter leaned over and whispered, "Something

weird is going on." He pointed toward the front of the bus.

"What do you mean? Things have been weird for a while." My head suddenly ached, and I rubbed the spot where Wybie had bumped me.

"Just look," Peter said, still pointing. All of our classmates were unaffected by the recent bump in the road that threw us out of our seats. "They're not moving."

He was right. They were frozen like statues. Since Mrs. Nebula was missing, it's not as if any of this could have been her doing.

"Weird. They're like zombies," I said. "Wonder why?"

"Not sure," Peter said. "But they're each holding a teddy bear."

"A teddy bear?" The hairs on my arms stood on end. "Mrs. Nebula, Mrs. Blackwood, Principal Geller...they were zombie-like..." It was all starting to add up and I didn't even like addition. "They all had teddy bears."

Peter's eyes grew wide. "What do you think—?"

"Would you look at that?" Bryce interrupted as he inched toward Wybie, gazing out the window.

Wybie's jaw dropped. "Whoa"

"The lights!" I shouted as I pointed out the window. "They're out!"

Peter jammed his elbow in my ribs. "Quiet! You don't want Ms. Martian to hear."

I lowered my voice to a whisper. "They're gone. I

can't believe it." Melissa stirred as I tapped her on the shoulder. "Heads up."

Melissa blinked. She sat up and leaned over a zombie-like kid in the seat next to her. She peered out the window. "Dang. What the heck happened?"

"Not sure. But I think we're about to find out." I gulped.

Melissa turned around to face me. "What makes you say that?"

"Just a hunch," I said as the bus approached the mouth of a tunnel. Two seconds later, the darkness swallowed us whole.

USE ALL OF YOUR SENSES

UNDERGROUND LAIRS AREN'T for the faint of heart.

1. They are dark.
2. They are cold.
3. They are empty.

Strange wails echoed around us. As the bus rolled to a stop, the cries grew louder. The driver parked in a shadowy recess of the cave, the headlights on the bus illuminating the otherwise dark cavern.

"What's that noise?" Wybie asked, his voice sounded scared even though I was sure he'd never admit it.

I wasn't going to admit it either. We were in a cave, with zombies for classmates, and a crazy person as our substitute. The noise certainly wasn't helping the situation. "Probably just the other kids on the bus." I squinted, adjusting my eyes to my dimly lit surroundings.

Bryce cleared his throat. "Since when do our classmates make those kinds of noises?" He blinked. Most likely holding back tears.

If tough guy was crying, then this situation was worse than I thought. I dug around in my backpack and pulled out a small penlight. The whole bus lit up like fireworks on the Fourth of July.

Blinded by the beam of light, Bryce shielded his eyes. "Watch it!"

"Turn that thing off," Melissa growled as she swung around in her seat to face me. "Ms. Martian will—"

"Will what, Melissa?" Ms. Martian stood inches away, tapping a foot. I shook my head and zipped my lips.

Melissa's cheeks puffed out as she held her breath. "Nothing." For some odd reason Melissa then winked at me. I winked back. Weirdo.

Ms. Martian's face glowed an eerie shade of green as I shined the light on her. "That's what I thought. Now children, I need you to be good students and cooperate with me." She placed one hand on her hip. The other she used to gesture at a row of kids. "Just look at how cooperative your class-mates have been."

"Yeah, and they're frozen like statues," Wybie blurted out.

Ms. Martian patted him on the head and his orange curls bounced. "Now, now, there's no harm that's been done."

No harm? They were zombies. If you could call that unharmed then, I guess, she was right. Otherwise, I was pretty sure there was something seriously wrong with them and I didn't want to be in their shoes. Cooperation was out.

"I have a gift for you," Ms. Martian said as she reached for my arm. "A very special gift. You'll just have to exit the bus to get it."

"No, thanks." I wasn't getting off this bus. Not in the dark. Not without my friends. And not with that crazy substitute! There was no way I would go into an unknown cave or wherever we were. It could be a monster's lair for all I knew. I most certainly wasn't putting myself in danger without some sort of protection. I just needed to find out what that was.

"Leave Doomy alone!" Melissa shouted.

Ms. Martian dropped my arm. "Didn't anyone ever teach you to respect your elders?"

Melissa smirked. "Not when they're nasty old women like you."

"Nasty, you say?" Ms. Martian threw her head back with a cackle. "You haven't even seen what I'm capable of."

"Stop picking on her." Peter stood up.

I cleared my throat. "Yeah, leave her alone."

Melissa shook her head and blinked. Was she trying to tell me something?

"More rude children? You'll talk to me with respect!" Ms. Martian made a sudden shift and instead of taking me, she grabbed Melissa by the arm. "And you're first."

"Why me?" Melissa furrowed her brow. She

looked angry, not scared. That girl wasn't afraid of anything.

"Ladies need to stick together. Don't we? That's the only way you'll learn to mind your manners." Ms. Martian might have been wearing a skirt, but I wouldn't have called her a lady.

"No thanks. I'd rather not." Melissa tried to jerk away but Ms. Martian was stronger than she appeared because she kept a tight grip. "Let go of me!" Melissa squealed but she also made a gesture with her hand, like she was holding a walkie-talkie. I knew right away that she had a plan. Sacrificing herself was part of it. "My dad will have you arrested!"

Ms. Martian tipped her head back as she laughed. "You can try but I assure you, he'll never find us here." Ms. Martian's voice had a hint of evil in it. By a hint, I mean a whole lot.

"Let go of her!" I stood up. My legs wobbled but I puffed out my chest so no one would see how scared I really was.

"Sit down," Ms. Martian said as she shoved me back into my seat. She pulled Melissa by the arm and dragged her toward the front of the bus. "You'll get your chance soon enough."

"Yeah, sit down, Doomy," Bryce said. "Your turn is next."

"Shut up." Wybie slugged Bryce's shoulder. "It's not really a turn we want to take," he mumbled through clenched teeth.

Melissa kicked and screamed as Ms. Martian dragged her down the aisle. She flailed about, gripping onto the seat backs. Ms. Martian yanked hard and Melissa's fingers slipped off the seat. Melissa wrestled to stay on the bus and when she reached out again, she grabbed a teddy bear instead. It broke free from one of our classmate's arms. Melissa immediately got a far off look in her eyes. She shook her head and dropped the bear almost instantly. "You'll never take me alive!' she screamed.

"Silly girl. I don't need you alive." Ms. Martian shoved a handkerchief in Melissa's mouth. "Now be a nice girl and keep quiet." She dragged Melissa down the stairs of the bus.

I glanced at Peter grasping at what to say. Then I saw the helpless expression on Melissa's face. "It'll be okay," I finally said.

"Make sure Doomy and his twerps don't escape," Ms. Martian said to Mr. Wooster who was in a catatonic state in the driver's seat.

"Yes, Ms. Martian," Mr. Wooster said as he swung the bus door closed, trapping us all inside.

We held our breath as we watched hopelessly. Deafening silence. That's what we heard for a second before I finally spoke up. "She sacrificed herself for us."

"How do you know?" Peter asked.

"She told me. I mean, she showed me." I made the same motion Melissa had made, like I had the much-needed device in my hand. "She's going to try to get the walkie-talkie."

The rest of the F.I.V.E.'s jaws came unhinged. No one was going to admit a girl outsmarted us. But I think we all felt lucky to have her on our team.

"Well, we can't just sit around and do nothing." Peter adjusted his glasses. He had a notebook in his lap and a pencil at the ready. "We need to make a plan."

"What kind of plan?" Bryce asked.

"A plan to make ice cream." I took the pencil from Peter and drew a circle.

Bryce licked his lips. "I like ice cream."

"He's joking, you dweeb. We're making an escape plan." Wybie had a pen and was jotting notes next to our drawing. "For someone whose dad was part of the experiment in Area 51, you sure are clueless."

"Shhhh...." I said, hearing a shuffling noise. "Listen." The beam of my penlight bounced around as I watched my classmates stir in their seats.

"They're moving." Peter's pencil slipped from his grasp and clattered to the floor.

"Quiet!" We needed to lay low for a while, just to be sure our classmates didn't try anything funny. "Too much noise might get their attention and they could turn against us."

"Yeah, they're zombies," Bryce said. "They might try to eat our brains."

"Don't worry. I think *you're* safe from that." Peter held back a snicker.

Suddenly, the bus driver stood up and made a zoned-out announcement. "Everyone off," he said as he pulled the lever and opened the bus door.

Our classmates stood up, each of them holding a bear. One by one, they began marching off the bus, single file.

A girl named Jennifer stumbled out of her seat. She dropped a teddy bear, paused, and turned to look at us. She blinked a few times. For a second it almost looked like she'd wake up from her zombie-like behavior. But then she picked up the teddy bear and hugged it tight to her chest. She immediately turned toward the front and resumed marching out the door of the bus.

"Whoa." My stomach churned seeing my classmate in such a trance. "Did you see that?"

"I think I did," Peter said.

"We better make a change to our plans."

"Doomy," Peter whispered as he tugged on my sleeve. "We've got to help Melissa get that walkie-talkie from Ms. Martian."

"And we need to take care of those bears," I said.

FOOL PROOF YOUR PLAN

WHEN MAKING A PLAN, it's important you think
it through.

1. Use a diagram.
2. Five everyone directions.
3. Keep a safe distance.

Peter, Wybie, and Bryce all fell into line behind me. Peter was too close, and he stepped on the back of my shoe, scraping my ankle. I felt the burn on my skin before I stumbled forward, landing face first on the floor by the bus driver's seat.

"C'mon guys." After the ache in my chin stopped, I scrambled to my feet.

"You're to stay right there," Mr. Wooster said in a spaced-out voice. He shoved me and I fell back into Peter. I was beginning to feel like a human ping-pong ball! Mr. Wooster exited the bus. When he reached the bottom of the stairs, he stood guard at the door, staring off into the dark.

Peter pushed into me again.

My legs felt unsteady and they almost gave way. "Watch it." I swung around and pointed the penlight in Peter's face.

"Sorry," Peter mumbled.

"What do we do now?" Wybie whined.

Peter pushed his glasses into place. "We go after them."

"Not so fast," Ms. Martian's voice screeched.

I shined my light out the door. Ms. Martian approached the bus, fists clenched, and teeth gritted together. "Quick," I said, stumbling toward the driver's seat. "Close the door!" I fumbled for the handle just as Ms. Martian reached the first step.

"What do you think you're doing?" she yelled.

Quickly, I yanked the lever. The door groaned as it slowly pulled to a close. "Locking you out." The lever was stiff, and the door refused to close all the way. Ms. Martian shot her hand into the bus. "A little help here," I hollered.

"I've got this," Bryce said, pulling the lever with ease. The door slammed, catching Ms. Martian's hand in the frame.

She screamed as she slipped free. "You little brats!" She shook a fist. Then she slugged Mr. Wooster in the gut. "What good are you?" Ms. Martian marched off into the cave, her body leaning so far forward I thought she'd fall face first into the ground.

"Thanks," I said high-fiving Bryce. But then I realized we were prisoners on this bus. We couldn't get out the front door or Mr. Wooster would grab us. The only other escape options were the windows, but that would be problematic. How would Bryce get his moose-like frame through those tiny openings?

I unzipped my backpack and searched for anything that might be able to help us. Pliers? Nope. Rope? Nah. Two bottles of Yoo-hoo. Eh. Might be good if we get thirsty. Hairspray. Eww! Each item I tossed aside Peter shoved in his bag. "What are you doing?"

"Thought maybe we could consolidate. No sense in having two bags."

"Smart." I nodded. "What do we do now?"

Bryce shrugged. "Looks like we're trapped."

I shined my light around the bus looking for an escape route.

Peter fell into a seat. "Maybe we just wait it out?" It was definitely a question even though his voice didn't go up on the end.

"Might as well make the most of it." Bryce grabbed a random lunch box and began eating a tuna fish sandwhich. "Must belong to Mikey Fuller." He tore off a bite with his teeth. "Not bad."

"Gross," Wybie said. "I can smell that all the way back here. Now we're trapped with fish odor."

I turned and shined my light on Wybie. That's

when I saw it. The emergency door. "Not quite." I pointed at the back of the bus.

"No way. Nuh-uh." Wybie hugged himself. "Not gonna happen."

"It's the only way out," Peter said.

"Wybie's afraid he'll break his arm again." I reached around Peter and put my hand on Wybie's shoulder.

"The teacher was supposed to catch me," Wybie said. "That jump is bigger than it looks."

My fingers gripped Wybie's shirt. "That happened in Kindergarden when you were shorter than my sister's can of hairspray. You're in fifth grade now. Pull yourself together."

"I'll go first," Bryce said as he rolled up his sleeves. "You can each jump down and use my back as a landing." He turned the lever and the emergency door on the back of the bus sprung open. He leapt out, landing on both feet like a gymnast.

"Great. I'll go next." Peter tossed his bag through the open door. He backed out and lowered himself to the ground. "C'mon, Wybie." He held his hand out.

Wybie peered down at the ground below. "That's a big nope."

"Let me go and then we can all help you." I brushed past Wybie and jumped. It was darker than I expected and so I didn't see Bryce kneeling on the ground like a human landing pad. He let out a loud umpf as I flattened him like a pancake.

"Watch it, Doomy," Bryce groaned.

"Sorry. I didn't know you were there." I quickly turned around and looked up at the back of the bus. "Where's Wybie?"

"How should I know?" Peter slipped his bag over his shoulders. "Didn't he jump out before you?"

"No." I shook my head. "He wouldn't do it. Thought if I went, it would encourage him."

Bryce stood up and peered into the bus. That guy was big. So big, in fact, he was waist level with the bottom of the door. "Wybie? Where'd you go?"

"Right here," Wybie squeaked.

"C'mon, you've got to jump." Bryce stood at the door. "Just scoot to the edge if you have to."

While they were trying to figure things out, I

watched my classmates march off to their doom. Turning quickly to Wybie I said, "Our friends are going to die. Either come with us now or stay behind on this dark, creepy bus all by yourself."

Wybie gulped. Then he jumped.

"Now let's go," Peter said helping Wybie to his feet.

"You okay?" Bryce grabbed Wybie's other hand.

Wybie nodded. "That wasn't so bad."

"Good. Because I have a feeling, things are about to get worse. See for yourselves," Bryce said as he pointed into the depths of the cave. It was nothing but utter blackness. Luke Skywalker had nothing on what we were about to venture into. "You go first, Wybie," Bryce said giving him a shove.

"Why me?" Wybie whined.

"Because you're annoying."

Wybie shoved a finger up his nose, plucked a goober, and flicked it at Bryce. "Am not!"

"Oh yeah?" Bryce puffed his chest.

"Shut up, you two! I'll lead." The shaking beam of light was a good distraction from the quiver in my voice. "Now, c'mon." We huddled together, staring into the darkness that crept on forever.

DIVIDE AND CONQUER

BEST MADE plans are laid to waste.

1. Throw everything out the window. Or the back of the bus.
2. Follow the screams.
3. Observe your surroundings.

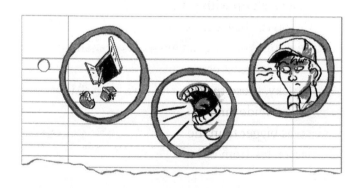

"Let's go this way," I said, as I started left.

Peter grabbed my arm. He pointed to the right where a teddy bear lay in the dirt. "I think they went *that* way."

"You're right. Let's go," I said, taking the first step. Once everyone fell in line behind me, the penlight illuminated our path, bouncing creepy shadows off the walls. Screams from our classmates sent shivers up my spine. Melissa needed to be okay or I'd never forgive myself.

As soon as we were deep in the cave, we saw our classmates heading down a large tunnel, it's opening like the mouth of a whale. "There they go!" I whispered. "You've got your bag, right, Peter?"

Peter nodded.

"And you know what to do, right, Wybie?"

"You got it, Captain."

I rolled my eyes. "Alright then. Bryce, you go left, and we'll catch up with you."

"I'm on it." Bryce took off in a jog.

We didn't know the layout of the cave, but we did know that like most caves, there would be tunnels. If you're lucky, those tunnels connect. Our plan was to split up. Divide and conquer and all that. Since Bryce was bigger than the rest of us, he could come at our classmates from one direction while we took the other.

"This way," I said, waving my arm. Our classmates weren't too far off, but if we didn't take action soon, they'd disappear into the depths of the tunnel for good.

"I'll follow you," Peter said, falling in step behind me.

"Where am I supposed to go?" Wybie called after us.

I stopped in my tracks and turned around. Wybie stood there with a confused look on his face.

"We just went over the plan." Something moved in the distance behind him. I shined my light toward it. "Oh no," I whispered, realizing two small red-eyed bears were headed our way. I couldn't let Wybie know what was behind him or he'd blow the plan. "You forgot already?"

"Uh." Wybie stared blankly.

I sighed loudly. "You're the bait."

"Oh right." Wybie nodded. "Wait. What?" His eyes grew huge. "When did I agree to that?"

"You didn't. But we've had a sudden change of plans." I pulled Peter's backpack off his shoulders and knelt on the damp ground as the bears marched closer.

"Why?" Peter crouched down next to me. "What's going on?"

I lowered my voice and whispered, "Killer bears at one o'clock."

"One o'clock?" Wybie questioned. "Why are you talking about time?"

"It's a location," Peter corrected. "Imagine the face of a clock and the time is the direction."

Wybie looked ahead and slightly off to his right—his one o'clock position. "I don't see anything except you guys and a few of our classmates."

"That's because it's your seven o'clock," Peter said, his voice quivering as he looked past Wybie and saw the bears for the first time.

"Shhh!" I sprayed spit everywhere. Peter was going to blow it!

Wybie turned around and gasped. "Are those..."

"BEARS!" Bryce screamed. He seemed to come from out of nowhere as he charged toward us. He sidelined Wybie as he blew past us still screaming.

"What do we do now?" Peter asked.

I rifled through his backpack. "Here." I handed

him my binoculars. "Use these. Tell me how many there are."

"Anyone ever tell you you're a nerd, Peterson?" Bryce said, slugging Peter's shoulder.

"Binoculars belong to Doomy. Guess he's a prepared nerd." Peter grabbed the binoculars and lifted them to his eyes. "At least three."

"There's four of us," I said zipping up the bag. "We'll be fine."

Peter cleared his throat. "Times ten."

"Thirteen?" Bryce raised an eyebrow.

"Thirty you dimwit. Three times ten is thirty." It struck me we were completely out-numbered and we'd never defeat an entire army of bears. We'd need to hide. It was our only option. I put the penlight in my mouth and started crawling across the cold, wet floor of the cave.

"What are you doing that for?" Wybie asked a little too loud. "Shouldn't we be running instead?"

"It's a combat crawl. We're not as easy to spot if we're on the ground." Bryce laid beside me. "I'll cover you."

I pulled the light out from between my teeth, aiming it at his face, so I could see his eyes. "You sure?"

"Yeah." Bryce pointed over my shoulder. "There's a tunnel just off to your left. Its narrow but I think we can fit. Better hurry before the bears reach us."

"Good plan," I said, feeling the chill on my stomach as I crawled. The light tapped against the ground with each move, causing the beam to bounce like we were on a ship. "You go first," I said to Wybie.

"Why do I always have to go first?"

"You don't doo-doo head. Doomy's led the way so far," Peter said. He shifted his backpack, which had rolled off to the side while he was crawling.

"You could be the bait instead," I reminded him.

Wybie shook his head. "Nah, it's good. I don't mind going first."

"That's what I thought." I figured all Wybie

needed was a little reminder. That'd get him to cooperate.

Peter grunted as he shifted the bag again. "Just get in there."

"And hurry up, would you?" Bryce said. "They're almost here." The soft sound of fluffy, furry stuffed animal paws told me he was right.

The tunnel was more like a crevice the size of a mouse hole. It was low to the ground, no wider than Bryce's shoulders, but very deep. Since it was so narrow, in order to escape quickly, we'd all need to be facing out. So Wybie scrambled into the slender opening feetfirst, followed by Bryce, then Peter. I crawled in last. We were stacked like chips in a tube of Pringles. A little too close for comfort.

"We made it." I breathed a sigh of relief.

There was a sudden sound of an out-of-tune tuba. Followed by a stench strong enough to wake the dead.

"Gross," Wybie said. "You farted in my face."

"Sorry." Bryce let another one rip. "That sandwich didn't settle well."

Wybie coughed. "You're disgusting."

"You're one to talk, boogerman," Peter said.

"Well you don't have your face in his rear end." Wybie made a gagging noise. "At least my boogers don't smell like a nuclear reaction."

"Nuclear reactions are odorless, you dimwit." Peter shifted, bumping into me.

"Careful," I said, turning just enough that I could look back at him. "And the rest of you be quiet."

"Uh, Doomy," Peter said, his eyes growing wide as he stared past me.

"What is it?"

Peter pointed. "Look."

I turned back around, shining my light out into the darkness. The army of identical teddy bears blocked the entrance of our tunnel, their beady red eyes glowing like orbs of evil.

NEVER SUBMIT TO ZOMBIFICATION

TEDDY BEARS SPELLED DOOM, not Doomy.

1. They controlled the minds of our friends.
2. They were just dumb stuffed toys.
3. They couldn't hurt us, not one bit.

The bear seized my arm. "Ahhhhh!" I shrieked. I didn't even care that I sounded like a little girl. That sucker had quite a grip. Plus I refused to submit to zombifcation. My penlight clattered to the ground and fizzled out. "It's got me!"

"Keep it down, Doomy." Peter grabbed my ankles. "*I've* got you."

Another fuzzy, red-eyed monster latched onto me. "No, a bear's got me!" Panic choked my throat and brain and I couldn't think. I scrambled out of the tunnel with a bear attached to each wrist. My eyes hadn't yet adjusted to the darkness and I decked Bryce in the nose as I tried to fling the bears off.

"Let me help," Peter said, still fumbling around in the dark.

"I got it." I flung my arms wide and the bears flew off my wrists. Phew!

The bus's headlights still offered a soft glow and I rubbed my eyes until I could see properly. Out of the darkness, two more bears came. They leapt into the air and latched onto my wrists where the first two had been. "They just keep coming!"

"It's a stuffed toy," Wybie said as he crawled out of our hiding spot and brushed the dirt off the knees of his jeans. "Just tear its arm off."

I fell to the ground, batting at the bears, trying to break free from their clutches. "I can't do that."

"You either have to take it down or it's going to take you with it." Peter pulled me by the ankles. My stomach burned as he dragged me against the cold, muddy floor of the cave. More bears latched onto the two attached to my wrists, forming a stuffed-animal chain.

"Doomy still sleeps with a teddy bear," Bryce said as he crawled alongside me.

"Do not." I denied it even though he was right.

"If you're not going to do it, I will." Wybie snatched the bear. Just as he was about to tear its limb off, he froze.

"Wybie." I grabbed the hem of his pants. "Are you okay?"

"Go away, Doomy." Wybie yanked his leg free and stumbled forward. He clutched the toy to his chest and zoned out just like I did during a history lesson. The bear controlled him, and Wybie headed off toward our classmates. When he reached them, he joined the end of the line. The group lurched forward, marching further down into the darkness of the cave.

"Wybie, get back here. You don't want to go with them." Peter was still hanging onto my ankles like I was a human wheelbarrow. "Let go of me." His grip loosened as I squirmed free and scrambled to my feet. "It's got Wybie."

"And we're surrounded." Peter huddled close.

"They just don't give up." Another bear clawed at my ankle. "I had no idea there'd be so many of them ready to launch an attack." A karate kick sent the bear deep into the tunnel.

Bryce picked up a stick and swung at one of the furry, little monsters. "Homerun!" The toy sailed through the air.

"We need to help Wybie." Sure, we needed to get out of our own mess first, but we couldn't just leave our buddy stranded. What if the zombie condition was permanent? We'd not only lose a member of the F.I.V.E.'s but we'd lose our friend, too.

"How do you propose we do that?" A bear threw itself at Peter who used his backpack as a shield. He kicked the toy, sending the red-eyed monster flying into a wall. "Everything we've tried has failed."

Bryce's makeshift bat made contact with another bear. "Yeah, got any other bright ideas, Doomy?"

He was right. They were both right. My ideas had all flopped. What happened to all the great planning my dad had taught me? So much for being a Prepper.

Bryce swung his stick again, but the bear grabbed it from his hands. His jaw went slack. "Did you see that?"

"Careful!" Another red-eyed monster charged from behind him. It crawled up Bryce's back and over his shoulder. Bryce grabbed it around the neck. "Don't touch it," I yelled, but it was too late.

Bryce zoned out, clutched the bear to his chest, and marched toward the other kids.

"Peter, we've got to think of something else." When I turned around, Peter was already grasping a bear in his arms. "No! No, no, no!"

My best friend in the whole entire universe stared straight ahead without blinking. Like I never even existed.

"Peter!" I grabbed him by the shoulders and shook him. He pushed me away and started marching with the group. "Don't let them take you!" But he didn't listen to me. He just kept obeying the monster's silent orders.

This was the end. Mind-controlling teddy bears had abducted all of my friends. I was helpless. If a single bear was capable of controlling one person, then this army would take me down like Superman exposed to kryptonite. But I couldn't just let my friends be at the mercy of these bears. I had no idea of what lurked at the bottom of the cave. There was no telling what would happen to them.

Peter's abandoned backpack laid on the floor. I slipped it on and raced after my friends, tripping as bears lunged at my ankles. More came at me, approaching from all directions. Some from behind, others from the side. They crawled up my legs. They squeezed my arms. One hugged my neck, choking me. I knew bear hugs were no good even if my mom tried to tell me otherwise!

Every time I shook them off, another came right back.

They were like moths to a flame.

Wait. That was it!

Firemen had come to our school last month.
They'd taught us how to survive if we were ever
caught in a fire. Stop, drop, and roll. That had to
work.

Quickly, I fell to the ground. "Stupid bears. You
can't hurt my friends and get away with it. I'll show
you who's boss!"

But as I rolled around, nothing changed. Bears

still clung to me. They crawled up my legs. The red-eyed monsters persisted.

"Guess the firemen's trick only works with fires." There was no other choice. I'd have to destroy them another way. Just as Wybie had suggested. A lump formed in my throat as I knew what I needed to do. Lifting a bear above my head, I said, "Let this be a lesson to you."

The bear wrestled to break free. My fingers gripped its arm, I closed my eyes tight, and ripped the bear's limb off. Then I tore off the other one, and both legs. I twisted its head and the red-eyed monster's eyes fizzled out. "I did it! I really did it."

Now that I knew what needed to be done, it didn't feel so bad, especially since I could help my friends. Sure, it brought back horrible visions of my neighbor's dog tearing my favorite stuffed teddy bear apart, but I'd have to shove that down deep and not think about it.

One by one, I tackled the bears, removing their limbs and twisting off their heads. A huge pile stretched out before me. Exhausted, hot, and sweaty, I leapt into the mound of stuffing, fluff, and fur. Something jabbed my ribs. Curious, I held the bear up and inspected the remains. Exposed in the seam was a tiny black box. "What on earth?" I slipped it in my pocket and darted off to catch up to my friends.

"Peter!" I grabbed his hand and pulled him from the group. "Wake up!" Then I did something I never thought I'd do, especially to my very best friend. I slapped him.

On the face.

Twice.

Peter moaned.

"C'mon, Peter. I know you're in there."

"M...m...move," Peter groaned.

"No, you move!" I pushed him. Hard.

Peter stumbled forward. He blinked. Then he resumed marching.

I tugged his arm and he jerked away. I yanked at the bear, but he gripped it tighter. "No, Peter! Don't go down there. It's a trap." It was no use. I couldn't seem to wake him, and I couldn't get the bear away. Then I suddenly realized something. How could the bears control everyone but me?

Peter, Bryce, and Wybie were all holding bears. The bears had practically smothered me, but they didn't control me like they did my friends. I'd just ripped them limb from limb, but nothing had happened. How was that even possible?

A dribble of sweat dripped from my forehead into my eyes. Using the hem of my shirt I dried my face, but knocked my baseball cap. When I placed it back on my head, that's when I felt it. The aluminum foil.

"That's it!" I whisper-shouted. "It's the foil. My dad was right!"

Which meant these teddy bears weren't just any

ordinary mind-controlling teddy bears. Oh no. They were *alien* mind-controlling teddy bears.

BECOME A MORSE CODE NINJA

EVERY DAY I learn something new about myself.

1. My friends meant more to me than pizza.
2. Teddy bears weren't so hard to destroy.
3. I was a great big, chicken.

"Let's get these monsters," I said as I stared into the dark, endless cave. Obviously, the mind-controlling source was in there somewhere since that's where everyone was headed. I didn't know what it was or what it intended to do with a bunch of fifth-grade students. I did know one thing. There was only one person left who could save them. That person was me.

I was about to grab Bryce's bear when Ms. Martian appeared in the distance. If she saw me, we were all doomed. But there wasn't time to escape. What would dad tell me? If you can't beat them, join them.

That's what I'd have to do.

"Just march in line with them." The lump in my throat scratched all the way down, like a piece of pizza crust that hadn't been dunked in cola. "Pretend you've been mind-controlled, too." With a shaky foot, I stepped in line and faked it as best as I could.

The sound of my own heartbeat thudded so loudly it nearly drowned out any other noises. As we stood in line awaiting our doom, Ms. Martian approached. My breath caught in my throat.

"I see you've joined us, Doomy." Ms. Martian hissed the words in my ear.

"Yes, Ms. Martian," I said in a monotone voice. My act needed to be convincing or she'd know I was faking. I didn't want to find out what would happen if she learned the truth. Playing it cool was the only way to survive.

"Good boy." Ms. Martian laughed. "Now it's time to get to work on this one." Ms. Martian tugged on a rope and Melissa stumbled forward. She still had the gag in her mouth but now her hands were tied, too.

"Doomy," Melissa mumbled through the gag.

I needed to let her know I was okay. But I had to do it without Ms. Martian catching on.

Ms. Martian turned her back and yanked Melissa by the hair. Melissa's muffled cries made me flinch. I felt awful that I'd let Ms. Martian take her so easily. I was a terrible friend.

Melissa made eye contact with me. Her eyes fell to my chest. I glanced down, noticing my empty arms and realized I'd made a very big mistake. No bear! If it came to Ms. Martian's attention, we were both done for.

Cupping my hands, I shrugged.

Melissa blinked.

I blinked back.

Ms. Martian whipped around, and I went into zombie mode with my hands at my side. "Hmmm..." She tapped a finger to her chin. Frozen in place, I could hardly breathe. My real teacher, Mrs. Nebula, had given me some good practice at this statue thing but even this was a bit much. "Did you just...?"

Melissa blinked again. It was strange, but I almost thought she was trying to communicate with me. She took a deep breath and screamed.

Ms. Martian turned around and struck Melissa's face. "Keep quiet!"

Melissa closed her eyes and took three steady breaths. A welt swelled up on her cheek.

My fingers curled into a fist. Ms. Martian would pay for hurting my friend.

Melissa glanced at my clenched hand and shook her head. She was right. Staying calm would protect us both right now.

Up ahead, someone stirred, dropping their bear

and stepping out of place. Ms. Martian stomped off mumbling something about keeping us in line.

With Ms. Martian's back turned, I blinked twice at Melissa. If she was trying to tell me something, I was going to do everything I could to help. She blinked three times and I repeated it. A series of short and long blinks followed.

Morse code.

I knew it! I should have clued in when she mentioned her dad's telegraph.

Lucky for her, my dad had taught it to me in one of our many prepping sessions. Melissa's dad was in the Navy before she was born. He must have taught her, too.

All those times I thought she was winking at me, weren't really winks at all. She was showing me she knew the special language.

"S-H-A-R-E-T-H-E-F-O-I-L," Melissa said in a series of blinks.

Share the foil! I touched my head remembering how Melissa saw the exposed foil during the bus ride. That was it! I could share the foil with my friends and then we could rescue our classmates. "W-E W-I-L-L H-E-L-P-Y-O-U," I blinked in response. First, I'd have to help Peter, Wybie, and Bryce and then the three of us would be able to take down Ms. Martian —and rescue Melissa—together.

Ms. Martian turned around sharply. She stormed up between us. Her gaze darted between Melissa and me. "I thought I saw..."

My eyes watered as I stared ahead, unblinking.

"Mm...Mmrrr..." Melissa mumbled through the handkerchief in her mouth.

"Be quiet," Ms. Martian ordered. "I'll handle you once and for all." She tugged Melissa's rope and the two disappeared back into the darkness.

I thought about the code Melissa and I exchanged in our blinks. This plan might just work. My dad had been right about aliens. The foil had protected me from their mind control. Dad had also taught me to trust others when they had a good plan. Melissa's idea was genius. If I was the only one with foil on my head, then I was the only one who could help. But if I shared the foil, there'd be four of us. So, I'd follow the plan. The best part? Melissa trusted me. I wasn't going to let her down.

My eyes zeroed in on the back of Peter's head who stood robotically, not moving. This was it. All or nothing. Peter would have to go down first and then we'd take the others together. I shoved into him and Peter fell to the ground with a groan. The bear toppled off to the side and I retrieved it, shredding it to pieces.

My classmate, Jennifer, stepped from her spot in line and stumbled backward. She looked possessed and I couldn't take any chances. So, I pulled the teddy bear from her arms and ripped the toy limb from limb. A pile of fluff lay at my feet.

Jennifer stared at the mound then she looked at me. Her eyes rolled and she promptly fainted.

"Doomy?" Peter sat up rubbing his head. "What happened?"

"Don't worry about that right now." I wanted to tell him everything, but there wasn't time. The basics would have to do. "Just promise you'll listen. I'm going to need your help."

"Sure. What can I do?"

"You can start by tearing the bears away from our classmates." I pointed at the line of kids marching into the darkness.

Peter nodded. "You got it."

"But you'll need some of this first." I removed my baseball cap and tore off a strip of aluminum foil.

Peter furrowed his brow. "What's this—"

"Don't ask."

"Aluminum foil, Doomy? I thought that was a joke."

"Just put it on."

"If you say so." Peter molded the foil to his head.

"And take this." I removed his backpack that I'd been carrying and held it out for him. He swiped it and slipped it on.

We ran up the line, working together as I took the bear from Wybie while Peter ripped the limbs off the toy. Wybie rubbed his eyes, looking only slightly worse for wear. "What did we miss?" he asked with a yawn.

"I found Melissa." I tried to catch my breath as I took another bear and ripped it apart. "I also defeated the army. Now we need to demolish the rest of them."

"Great." Wybie reached for a bear. "Count me in!"

"Don't touch it!" I shouted too loudly, and it echoed around us.

Wybie recoiled. "Why not?"

"Because it'll control you again." I ripped the bear from Bryce's arms and tossed it to Peter.

"Then how's Peter touching it?" Wybie asked still a bit groggy.

I lifted my hat and pointed to the shiny silver stuff on my head. "The foil."

Bryce woke up and stared at me blankly.

"Don't worry, Bryce," I said. "Everything will be just fine." I gave him and Wybie a piece of foil to protect their brains from the mind-controlling teddy bears. "No questions. Just wear it." They quickly molded it against their heads and got to work.

We inched our way down the line. Each of us taking a bear from our classmates and ripping it limb from limb. As we got deeper into the tunnel, an eerie glow began to illuminate the cave.

"I don't like the looks of this." I glanced ahead into the cavern where the light bounced shadows off the walls.

"Me either." Peter ripped a head off a bear. He studied it a second before tossing it aside.

As we rounded the corner, we saw where the line ended. Or, rather, where it began. All of our classmates were single file. Some of the missing adults were in line, too, including Mrs. Blackwood and Principal Geller.

They marched straight up a ramp into the mouth of a silver crescent.

It had the same flashing lights as the ones above our town.

The same lights we'd been told never to look at.

The same lights we'd been told never to question.

The same lights we'd been told never to speak of.

The lights of a spaceship.

21

BE SMARTER THAN YOUR AVERAGE TENTACLE

ALIENS HAVE MORE than one trick up their sleeve.

1. Teddy bears are just the decoy.
2. Mind control is only the beginning.
3. Trusted adults would never be their weapon.

"Doomy Prepper," a woman's voice said.

"Mrs. Nebula?" I cried aloud as I saw her standing on a metal balcony. She leaned against the railing, peering down at us. "What a relief it is to see you!" Never thought I'd ever say those words.

Mrs. Nebula lifted her arm, holding it straight out with her hand curled. The lights from the spaceship created a long, skinny shadow which raised up on the wall beside her. At her side, a teddy bear dangled from the fingertips of her other hand.

"We did it!" Wybie kicked the mound of stuffing as he ran toward us. The fluff flew up into the air and gently rained down. It landed on a few rescued classmates who were sound asleep on the ground.

"Not quite," I said with a pant. "Mrs. Nebula has a bear." My finger pointed at her like a guided missile. "We need to help her—"

"Hush boy." Mrs. Nebula rotated her hand. Another long, skinny shadow slithered up the wall. I squinted and suddenly realized it wasn't a shadow after all. It was a tentacle!

"Watch out!" The thing climbed the wall of the cave beside Mrs. Nebula who seemed unalarmed. She turned her hand again and as I watched her, I felt something slither across my shoe. I glanced down. Another tentacle!

Before I could move, it squeezed around my waist. I couldn't breathe. "Some help over here, please." The words came in a grunt as the tentacle squeezed tighter.

Its suction-like cups stuck to me as it lifted me higher and higher into the air. Mrs. Nebula, my mind-controlled fifth grade teacher, had manipulated this thing into a death trap. My limbs were too weak to fight. It was useless. My body fell limp. Oxygen is kind of a vital thing. Without it, well, you die.

Wybie punched the octopus-tentacle but it only tightened its grip.

"Not him." Peter pointed at the balcony where Mrs. Nebula stood. "Get her."

"Mrs. Nebula?" Bryce scratched his head.

"If we remove the threat and free Mrs. Nebula of the mind-control, then the tentacle will release Doomy." Peter adjusted the straps of his backpack.

Mrs. Nebula's eyes began glowing red, just like the ones on the teddy bears. She acted like Darth Vader, using some unseen force to control the monster. Her hand twisted and turned, as she forced the tentacle to lift me even higher into the air.

"Don't worry." Wybie dashed toward our teacher. "I've got this." He climbed the metal stairs leading to the balcony.

A tentacle slithered behind him. "Look out!" My voice was weak. Nearly all my air had been squeezed out.

The creature's limb curled around Wybie's ankle. It yanked him from the stairs and raised him all the way up to the ceiling. He swung there like a pendulum.

Bryce balled his hands into fists and began punching the tentacle that held me captive.

"Let's go." Peter waved at Bryce who sprinted ahead to catch up with him.

"I'll be back," Bryce said as he glanced over his shoulder. A tentacle came from out of nowhere, crashing down right in front of Bryce. He hopped over it and kept running.

Another one shot out and nabbed Peter. He squirmed but was trapped just like me and Wybie.

Mrs. Nebula laughed as she controlled a fifth

tentacle. It lifted high above Bryce's head then smacked hard against the ground, narrowly missing my friend. Two more tentacles waved about, but Bryce sailed past them both.

An eighth tentacle appeared behind the spaceship. In it was Melissa. The gag had been removed from her mouth, but she was so lifeless, she looked like a ragdoll as the tentacle bounced her about.

Bryce never stopped running, dodging the four free tentacles. He climbed the ladder and tackled Mrs. Nebula. She hit her head and didn't move. Bryce dismantled the bear in three seconds flat.

The tentacle around my waist loosened and I fell to the ground in a loud thud. Gasping for air, I ignored the pain in my side. Peter and Wybie were free, too.

Bryce carried Mrs. Nebula down the ladder and placed her on the floor of the cave. After a few minutes she rubbed her head and sat up.

"Doomy?" Mrs. Nebula looked around the darkened cave. "Peter? Wybie?"

"And me," Bryce said.

"Plus, Melissa." I tipped my head where our friend lay unconscious near the opening of the spaceship. "And pretty much the entire fifth grade and the Catskill region." It might have been a slight exaggeration.

"Where are we?" Mrs. Nebula climbed to her feet.

"We've been abducted by aliens," I said matter-of-factly.

Mrs. Nebula smiled at the four of us. "You saved me, didn't you?"

"I guess you could say that." I shrugged.

"Don't be so modest." Mrs. Nebula stumbled toward me and rubbed the top of my baseball cap. "You're a good boy, Doomy." She pulled me to my feet and wrapped me in a big hug.

Normally, that would have been super embarrassing. The truth was, I didn't mind. I'd never been happier to have my teacher back. Even if she was hugging me in front of my friends.

"We're not done yet." Wybie pointed to a line of classmates boarding the ship.

"We need to finish this," Peter said.

Mrs. Nebula went pale as she stared at the spaceship. "I don't feel so good, Doomy." She wobbled a bit and I steadied her by the elbow so she wouldn't fall.

"Sit here." I helped lower her to the ground. "I have something that will help." I rifled through Peter's backpack for the Yoo-hoo. When I turned to hand it to her, she threw up. And then she promptly fainted.

"Guess that means we're on our own," Wybie said.

"What are we going to do now?" Bryce threw his hands into the air.

"I'm going to take care of Melissa," I said, bringing

the Yoo-hoo with me as I went to her side. She had a pulse and, although her breathing was shallow, she looked like she'd be okay. I placed the drink next to her and returned to the group. We still had work to do.

Peter knelt down and started tossing things out of his backpack. He held up two cans of WD-40.

"What's that for?" Wybie scratched his head.

"It's good for oiling hinges and stuff," Bryce said. "Seen my dad use it around the house." He paused. "Hey, Peterson, why you got that in your bag, anyway?"

"It's for a project," Peter said.

I patted Peter's shoulder. "Yeah, he's building a computer."

"Technically, it's a robot." Peter pushed his glasses into place.

I knelt down beside him. "So, what are we going to do with that stuff?"

"We're going to grease the tentacles." Peter tossed me a can. "And then we win."

DEFEAT THE RIGHT ENEMY

A GIANT ALIEN, octopus-creature wasn't so hard to defeat.

1. It only had eight legs.
2. It wasn't too sticky.
3. It was outnumbered four to one.

"The F.I.V.E.'s are back," Melissa said as she ran toward us.

"You're okay!" I hugged her but then pushed away. Hugging a girl was gross. I couldn't let her think I liked her or something.

"Yeah." She rubbed her head where a big bruise had formed. "I'll be fine."

Her plan to share the foil was perfect. I only hoped she'd been just as successful in her mission. "Did you take care of Ms. Martian?"

"You bet I did. All thanks to your plan and some well-timed escape acts." Melissa smiled as she dusted her hands off. "Let's just say Ms. Martian is all *tied up*."

"And thanks to yours." I pointed to the mound of teddy bear parts. "We stopped the mind control."

"Well, for most of them." Peter motioned at the line of students still boarding the spaceship.

"Enough already," Wybie said as he headed closer to the ship. "We've got bigger fish to fry." Behind the spacecraft was the largest alien creature I'd ever laid eyes on. Its head was the size of two hot air balloons. It's eight tentacles stretched out across the floor of the cave, a few of them snaking their way into different tunnels.

"Calamari," Bryce said.

"That's squid, you doo-doo head." Peter pulled the cap off his can of WD-40. "Cooked octopus is just octopus. Cooked squid is calamari."

"Besides, I'm not going to cook it," I said, uncapping my can. "We're just going to grease it."

"Smart thinking." Melissa folded her arms in approval. "I'll do the cooking." She pulled a lighter from her pocket and flicked it on.

"Now, let's get to work." Peter aimed the nozzle toward the suction cups on the alien creature's tentacles as he marched toward the spaceship.

Melissa and I jogged down another tunnel where we found two tentacle-arms. They wiggled and writhed. She stepped around it like a super hero. In fact, she kind of was. When I followed her lead, my shoe got wedged and I tripped. The tentacle sprung to life and instantly grabbed Melissa. It wrapped around her middle. The thing started to squeeze, and Melissa gasped.

"Help!" Her weak scream came out as a whisper.

I quickly sprayed the limb and Melissa slipped from its grasp.

"Worked like a charm. Thanks." She high-fived me.

"No problem. Now, let's take care of this fish-head once and for all." I pressed the nozzle and a stream of oil coated the alien's limb.

Melissa flicked on her lighter. She held it close to the tentacle and it burst into flames. Horrible screeching cries came from the monster.

"Let's get out of here." A flaming tentacle whizzed past, just missing my shoulder. Sparks and flames rained down.

"Maybe the lighter wasn't such a great idea," Melissa said. "The whole cave could catch on fire. Or worse," she paused and whispered, "explode."

"Too late for that now," I said as I sprayed oil on another tentacle while racing back into the main lair where the giant fish-head watched from behind the spaceship. I skidded to a stop when I saw its face. "Would you look at that?"

The creature's four large eyes stared in our direction. It opened its mouth, exposing rows of razor-sharp teeth as it wailed again. The arms moved erratically as the creature curled them in from the tunnel chambers into the lair. The fiery tentacle fizzled out. Puffs of smoke lifted to the ceiling.

"It's angry," Melissa said.

"I would be, too. At least the fire's out. Now we don't have to worry about being blown to smithereens." Maybe I could have phrased it better because Melissa gave me a strange look.

"Watch out!" Peter cried as he came running toward us. A tentacle slithered behind him. It suddenly lifted into the air and smashed against the wall of the cave. Dirt and rocks rained down. Peter looked up at the large crack that had formed. "We need to do this fast. Or we're all going to die beneath a pile of rubble."

"I'm trying," I said, weaving around flailing tentacles. The alien creature howled as it lifted its arms, and then slapped them against the ground. It curled them into its body then shot them out like a party horn. One came straight at me. I ducked just as it sailed overhead. Another came from behind. The arm wrapped around my middle, squeezing me tight.

I'd been in this predicament before. Thankfully, I had a tool to help me this time. A thick layer of grease coated the suction cups as I sprayed the can of WD-40. Slipping free, my neck caught between two suction cups. My body dangled beneath me. The tentacle tightened, squeezing until my head felt like a pimple about to explode.

Melissa stomped on the alien's appendage, and the creature made a high-pitched screech. The can slipped from my hands and rolled to Melissa's feet. She sprayed the WD-40 on the tentacle and I finally slipped free, falling to the ground. "Take that," Melissa said, kicking the alien.

The creature wailed again, and my friends all dropped to their knees, covering their ears.

"Kill it!" Wybie yelled. He scrambled to his feet, hands still on his ears, and joined Melissa as the two of them kicked the creature.

The alien whipped a limb like it had taken lessons from Indiana Jones. Melissa quickly darted out of the way. It made contact with Wybie who went flying. He smashed against the wall of the cave and landed hard.

"You can't do that to my friend," Bryce said as he charged at the monster and climbed up to the top of its head. He beat his fists into its flesh. With each blow, the tentacles flailed. Slimy green goo splattered everywhere. I wanted to hurl.

The alien-monster blinked.

Once.

Twice.

Long then, short.

I gasped. Then I blinked back.

The alien blinked again, his tentacles writhing as Bryce punched it.

A long blink, then a short one. Two more. Then Three.

"Stop," I cried as I ran toward Bryce. "Stop, stop!"

"He hurt Wybie," Bryce cried through sobs.

"It's trying to communicate," I said.

"I saw it, too." Melissa ran up beside me. "Morse code."

"Exactly." I slipped my hand into hers. "An experiment?" I repeated as the alien told its story. It blinked again. "It wants help."

"Quick. Ms. Martian is tied up over there," Melissa said pointing to her left.

Ms. Martian sat in a corner on the opposite side of the spaceship, a gag in her mouth, and rope around her wrists and ankles. "Impressive."

Melissa smirked. "You're not the only one who's been prepped."

A surge of pride hit me. This girl was okay in my book. "You think she still has the walkie talkie?"

"I know she has it." Melissa squinted. "I tried to get it from her after I tied her up, but the alien grabbed me first."

"What are we waiting for?"

Melissa's hand was still in mine and she squeezed it before running off toward the substitute. I sprinted to catch up with her. Ms. Martian squirmed and mumbled, looking a bit like a fish out of water as she flopped around.

"Turnaround is fair play." Melissa grabbed the walkie talkie from Ms. Martian's purse. Once it was in her hand, she acted like she was going to slap her. Ms. Martian flinched. "Don't worry. A lady would never slap someone."

"Mmm...mrrr," Ms. Martian mumbled through the gag in her mouth.

"What is it, you old hag?" I pulled the gag from her mouth.

"You can't take that walkie-talkie!" Ms. Martian snarled.

"Try and stop me.' I shoved the gag back into her mouth, noticing that her make-up had worn off. Her lizard-like skin wasn't just creepy, it was gross. "You really are green."

"From the experiment," Melissa said. She handed me the walkie-talkie. "I believe this is yours."

The dial clicked as I turned it to channel four. "Dad," I shouted into the walkie. "Dad? Can you hear me?"

"Doomy?" Static buzzed through the speaker nearly drowning out my dad's voice. "Doomy! Yes, son. I can hear you!"

My hand shook as I said, "Experiment 362."

NEVER TRUST AN ALIEN THAT SAYS IT COMES IN PEACE UNLESS YOU WANT TO BECOME ITS PIECES

MARTIANS COME in all shapes and sizes and they all just want to eat us.

1. Some are giant.
2. Some are small.
3. They are all scary.

Three cute little alien creatures slithered out from behind a rock. Each one like a miniature slimy octopus with big doe eyes. "Aliens!" Bryce screamed as he pointed at them.

I nodded but watched as the big octopus alien blinked more of its story.

A few other tiny alien creatures crept toward Peter. "There's more!" he cried, putting his hands up in defense.

"They're just babies," Melissa said.

Ms. Martian mumbled again.

"Not babies." I blinked at the creatures. They blinked back. "They're adults."

"What do they want?" Bryce slid down from the giant octopus head.

The creatures blinked at me. Long, short. Blink, blink, blink.

"They just want to go home." I kind of felt bad for them.

Peter dropped his can of oil. "You mean they're trapped here?"

"I think so." I knelt down, getting eye level with the pint-sized creatures. I put my hand out and the alien slithered onto my palm.

"Careful." Wybie limped toward us. "They might bite."

"No," Melissa said, blinking at the small aliens. "They don't want to harm us."

"Don't want to harm us?" Bryce snorted. "What do you call that?" He pointed at the giant fish-head creature who tried to strangle us. Its wounded tentacle arms were curled up close to its body. The one we'd set on fire looked like Sunday night's pot roast.

"It was Ms. Martian's doing," I said, interpreting the Morse code blinks from the creatures.

"Mmhmmhmm," Ms. Martian mumbled through her gag.

"How do you explain the spaceship?" Wybie, clearly upset, threw his arms in the air. "And our zombie-classmates? And the mind-controlling teddy bears?"

"Mm...hmm...mm," Ms. Martian tried to say.

"Shut up." Bryce pointed a finger at her.

"Let her talk." Peter walked over and removed her gag. "We all deserve an explanation."

"You stupid kids!" Ms. Martian screamed. "You ruined everything! If only—"

Peter shoved the gag back into her mouth. "Bryce was right. Shut up."

"She was bartering," I said, watching the small aliens blink their story to me.

Melissa gasped and started shivering. "Ms. Martian was sending our classmates in exchange for the octopus. Adults, too."

"Why would she do that?" Wybie took off his coat and placed it on Melissa's shoulders.

"To keep them satisfied." Melissa's teeth chattered. "One human for one more day with the alien octopus."

"A life for a life." Peter lowered his head.

"But the aliens just wanted to take their friend home. They didn't want any part of this." I shook my head, unable to believe the story that was unfolding. "You can go home now," I said to the aliens in a series of blinks. "It's all over."

The alien squirmed out of my hand and inched its way up the ramp. Two dozen others crawled out from their hiding places along the wall of the cave. They inched their way aboard the spacecraft.

We followed close behind and stopped when we reached the wide-mouthed entrance. The spacecraft's lights flashed, and the remaining teddy bears fell to the ground. Our classmates stumbled and then collapsed on top of each other.

"They killed them!" Bryce shouted. "They're liars!" He bolted up the ramp of the spaceship, fists at the ready.

"No, no, no!" I called as I ran after him. "It's okay. They're just deactivating the bears."

"They'll all wake up in a minute," Melissa said. "See for yourself."

Kristy Bradshaw was the first one to open her eyes. She sat up, rubbed her face, and looked around.

"It's okay Kristy." Peter ran over and helped her to her feet. "You've just been abducted by aliens. They were taking you to another planet for experiments but you're safe now."

"What?" Kristy swayed in place and just as she was about to faint, Peter caught her.

"That was stupid," Wybie said. "Even I knew better than to tell her something like that."

"Stupid, eh?" Peter lowered his glasses. "Watch this."

Kristy gasped for air, opened her eyes, and looked at Peter. They held a gaze. Then she threw her arms around his neck. "My hero!"

Peter grinned. He glanced my way and winked.

NEVER TAKE ALL THE CREDIT

HEROIC DEEDS WERE OVERRATED.

1. There was praise.
2. People cried.
3. Kissing wasn't allowed.

Melissa kissed my cheek. "You're a hero, Doomy."

"Nah. Not really." I wiped the kiss away. I couldn't let her know that, secretly, I kind of liked it. "Besides, we did it together."

Melissa blushed. "I guess we did, didn't we?"

The police cuffed Ms. Martian and loaded her into the back of their patrol car. "We've been after this one for a while," the officer said. "Your smart thinking will have her behind bars for a long time." The officer patted Melissa on the shoulder.

"Do you know why she did it?" someone in the crowd shouted.

The officer put pen to paper. "Experiment gone wrong. Had to take it out on somebody."

An official looking man in uniform stepped between them. "Never mind that," he said. "That's a need-to-know basis only and you don't have a need to know."

Except, little did *he* know, the F.I.V.E.'s already knew the truth. Ms. Martian wanted to continue her experiments on the creature. She needed to barter real-live humans in exchange for each day she kept the alien-octopus imprisoned. It was her only way to conduct more experiments. It was terrible. What was worse, Ms. Martian didn't care who she hurt, human or alien.

"Well, maybe you can do something for her skin." I gestured to her green, lizard-like face.

"Afraid it's permanent," the man said. He blinked like he had revealed too much.

"It all had to do with the experiment," Melissa whispered. "I read up on 362 when Bryce showed you the document. She'd been testing different chemicals on the alien and the creature began doubling in size. When he grew, his arms knocked over the chemicals. They spilled on Ms. Martian and left her scarred for life."

Another patrol car arrived, its lights flashing and sirens blaring. The police officer opened the back door and my parents leapt from the vehicle.

"Doomy!" my mom cried as she rushed toward me, tackling me in a hug.

Dad removed my hat and the aluminum foil fluttered to the ground. He ruffled my hair. "Proud of you, son."

"Thanks, Dad."

"I knew it, Doomy. All this time! I knew it!" Dad wiped sweat from his brow, but it was really just to hide the fact that he was dabbing away a tear.

"Well, I'm just glad I was prepared." Mom held out a roll of toilet paper for Dad who tore off a piece and blew his nose. "You never know when you're going to need it. Right, Doomy?" Mom winked.

I winked back. "Totally."

A reporter hurried up to us. "Alex Shovan with Channel Nine News," he said shoving the microphone in my face. "Care to tell us how you defeated the creature?"

Peter, Wybie, and Bryce walked up alongside me, each of them wrapped in heavy blankets.

I smiled at them, then I spoke clearly into the microphone. "With a little help from my friends." It was true. The F.I.V.E.'s helped. We all did. More important, they were my friends.

As commotion swirled around us—reporters, police, firemen, paramedics, bystanders—the lights began to flash. "Look!" I pointed. "The lights."

Everyone stopped talking and, for the first time, gazed up at the sky. They were unafraid, thanks to the F.I.V.E.'s. We were free to look at the lights, to talk about them, and to acknowledge they'd been there for far too long. Ms. Martian had done this to our town. She'd created the fear. Our distrust. But it was over now.

Smiling, I surveyed the crowd who watched in awe as the lights changed from white to green to pink, then back to white.

The lights blinked.

Once, twice.

Long, short.

Dad's jaw dropped. "Would you look at that!"

"They're going home." I folded my arms, satisfied I'd helped the creatures.

The lights suddenly went out. The crowd gasped. Then, one by one, the lights began to glow again. First, the one in front. Then the one next to it, and the next, until they were all lit up. They grew so bright I could hardly look at them. Then the spacecraft began to twirl, faster and faster. The lights became one giant blur. The silver crescents whirled in the sky and then, in an instant, they were gone.

"Morse code," Melissa whispered.

"Sure is." I nodded. Then I smiled to the sky and blinked back. "You're welcome."

ACKNOWLEDGMENTS

Thank you to my family for their patience as I worked to bring this story to life. Their encouragement meant so much. You can imagine my surprise when I saw my husband standing in the background waving his hands as he did some ultimate cheerleader moves, minus the pompoms. The cheering was a bit loud but I excused it on account that he brought chocolates and flowers.

It goes without saying that I owe my beta readers, my intern, Josie, and my editor, Tim a world of thanks. You took my clunker and turned it into a luxury sedan. I couldn't have done it without you.

Many thanks to my readers who are some of the most awesome people on planet Earth!

A NOTE FROM THE AUTHOR

Doomy has lived in my head for many, many years. Back in 2012, before Cinderskella was ever published, I'd had the idea for a story about a family obsessed with preparing for the apocalypse. My experience with the panic of Y2K led me to my own efforts in personal food storage (chocolate) and emergency preparedness (books). Over the years, I'd heard stories of families who were saving strange items in preparation for an emergency. This lead me to envision a fictional family that was a bit eccentric. Of course, their name needed to be a little different, too. Hence, Doomsday Prepper was born.

When I first set out to write Doomy, the story began with a zombie apocalypse (hang tight - that's next!) but realized, thanks to a fabulous editor, the story deserved a better starting point. What I also didn't know in my first drafts was the story needed a better setting. I drew upon some of my own childhood experiences including favorite films and icons, and knew I'd found the perfect place for Doomy to reside; 1986.

Doomy holds a special place for me as an author. He represents that perseverance and persistence needed so you never give up on your dreams. He taught me that it's okay to be prepared for the end of the world, too. Even if your stockpile is toilet paper.

I hope you enjoyed reading Doomy Prepper's adventures as much as I enjoyed writing them! There's nothing better than matching readers with great books. If you enjoyed this book, please leave an honest review. Reviews help authors find new readers.

AMIE BORST

ABOUT THE AUTHOR

Amie Borst believes in unicorns, loves glitter, and keeps a stash of chocolate hidden away from her chocolate-stealing family. She is the author of several books for children including the *Scarily Ever Laughter* series (*Cinderskella, Little Dead Riding Hood, Snow Fright*), the *Unicorn Tales* series, and the *Doomy Prepper* series. She is a judge on *Rate Your Story*, and a former founding member of the group blog, *From the Mixed-Up Files of Middle-Grade Authors,* where she contributed for nearly a decade. Visit her website for more information. While you're there, be sure to sign up for her newsletter so you can receive updates on new books, sales, and promotions.

Website: www.amieborst.com

ABOUT THE ILLUSTRATOR

Sean Bova is an American artist working and living in Southern California. He has been professionally illustrating a wide range of fiction, from children's books to sci-fi comics and horror novels, for several years. He studied art at California State University Long Beach, graduating from the art program with a specialization in illustration. Pen and ink remains his favorite medium although he also enjoys using digital art programs.

When not playing video games, Sean spends his time thinking about whether scientists could ever create a robot ninja. He is currently developing an original comic book while continuing to work on the Doomy Prepper series.

ALSO BY AMIE BORST

Scarily Ever Laughter series

Cinderskella

Little Dead Riding Hood

Snow Fright

Doomy Prepper series

Stay Tuned!

There's more to come!

Made in the USA
Middletown, DE
09 April 2020

88422717R00111